A Mirthful Wish

WISHING FOR LOVE

KRISTY MCCAFFREY

Also by Kristy McCaffrey

Historical Western Romances

The Wings of the West Series

The Wren

The Dove

The Sparrow

The Blackbird

The Bluebird

The Songbird (Novella)

Echo of the Plains (Short Story)

The Starling

The Canary

The Nighthawk

The Swan (Coming Soon)

Standalone

Into The Land Of Shadows

Historical Western Romance Short Stories

The Crow Brothers Collection

The West: A Romance Collection

Contemporary Western Romances

Blue Sage

The Peppermint Tree

A Mirthful Wish

Sweet Historical Romances

Rosemary

Alice: Bride of Rhode Island

Contemporary Adventure Romances

Deep Blue

Cold Horizon

Ancient Winds

Shark Reef

Sapphire Waves

A Mirthful Wish

Cover Design: No Sweat Graphics & Formatting

Editor: Mimi The Grammar Chick

Author Photo: Katy McCaffrey

E-book ISBN-13: 978-1-9528013-3-4

Print ISBN-13: 978-1-9528013-4-1

http://kmccaffrey.com/

kristy@kmccaffrey.com

One

[Don't miss "The Reindeer That Got Away," a digital prequel short story about Liam and Ellie. Find more info at kmccaffrey.com/the-reindeer-that-got-away/]

Early December

Liam Adler buttoned his coat as he walked down the main street in Barstow, an icy wind freezing his cheeks. Cold weather didn't normally bother him, but he'd forgotten how different winter days in Colorado could be from Pennsylvania.

In the distance, he caught sight of Ryan entering a storefront. Since it was mid-morning, Liam guessed his youngest brother was on a coffee break from the office Adler Inc. kept in Barstow. When the destination turned out to be Bella's Bakery, his assumption proved correct.

The establishment looked new, but Liam hadn't really spent any time in Barstow recently except for skiing at the resort, and despite being in town the last four weeks he hadn't paid attention to the local businesses. The arduous task of finding a new normal after the sudden death of his father had consumed each day. His middle brother, Flynn, had fled back to California as soon as the funeral had ended, leaving Liam and Ryan to face the cutting grief of their mother each day.

He entered the bakery as Ryan was taking a seat at one of the small tables with a hot drink and pastry in hand. A handful of customers sat at the other tables, a festive Christmas vibe filling the air, and for a moment Liam felt joy rather than sadness.

The young dark-haired proprietress behind the counter looked like Bella Thatcher. The last time Liam had seen her was at the Reindeer Ball five years ago. It was also the last time he'd seen her cousin, Ellie. He'd pretended to be Ellie's date to save her from the unwanted advances of Mark Osborn, a local boy Liam had never liked.

Liam knew the moment Bella recognized him because her amiable expression turned into a glare.

"Hi, Bella," Liam said with a smile and a nod. He wanted to ask about Ellie: What was she up to? Had she finished art school and traveled abroad? Was she married?

There had been a time when his mother had known such details, but even she had lost track of the Thatcher kids over the past few years.

"I'm sorry about your father," Bella said, her face softening with sympathy. "And I'm not trying to turn away business, but are you both trying to ruin mine?"

"You sold me the coffee," Ryan said in his defense, but there was humor in his voice.

A blush crept onto Bella's face, and she busied herself with something behind the counter. Liam looked at his brother and then at Bella and then back to Ryan.

He took a seat and said in a low voice, "Don't let Gramps see you come in here."

"You worry too much about what he thinks," Ryan said, stirring cream into his coffee as his Adler blue eyes flashed in irritation. Liam and Ryan took after their mother with their blond hair, but the eye color was all from Theo Adler, patriarch of the family.

Despite a family feud between the Adlers and the Thatchers—courtesy of the grandfathers—it hadn't kept Liam and his brothers from interacting with Ellie's brothers, Jamie and Owen, and Bella's brother, Mason, through the years. Or Liam with Ellie herself.

"Gramps would cut you out of the will as well as Adler Inc. if you so much as dated a Thatcher, let alone got serious, and God forbid, married one."

"You're moving awfully fast," Ryan murmured as he sipped his drink.

"How long have you been eating pastries? Weeks? Months?"

Ryan sighed. "Too long. I need to start working out more."

"If you two get serious, you'll need to leave the country, you know. And she's not leaving Reindeer Pass." It was clear that Bella's Bakery was a labor of love. There were too many special touches to doubt that.

"Thanks as always for your burning insight," Ryan said, a sarcastic tone in his voice. "And we're currently in Barstow."

Liam chuckled quietly, welcoming the brief amusement of teasing his brother, as if life were as normal as ever and not turned upside down by the loss of their dad.

Barstow was adjacent to Reindeer Pass. Ryan's argument was weak, and his brother knew it. The Adlers and Thatchers first settled in Reindeer Pass over a hundred years ago, and their descendants still lived there today—namely Bella and Ellie's parents as well as Liam and

Ryan's mom, and of course the grandfathers and their wives.

"Now I know why you didn't want to take over Adler Inc," Liam said. "You want an escape route so you can date a Thatcher."

Ryan glanced in Bella's direction. "Maybe."

Liam grabbed a piece of the cranberry tart from his brother's plate and asked, "When do you plan to make your move?" He suppressed a moan as the sugary food melted in his mouth. "Damn, this is good."

"I know," Ryan agreed. "And I've been trying to work up the nerve, but Bella's dislike of Adlers is well known."

"She's just been scared into it like the rest of us." Liam suspected her grandfather was as bad as theirs in stoking the ongoing feud. "You'll never know unless you ask her out, but if she says yes, I wouldn't advertise it in case it goes nowhere. No reason to cause any more stress in the family."

The shadowed cast of his brother's gaze reflected Liam's own grief.

Liam had been in town since Thanksgiving to support his mom, who had been reeling after losing his dad in early November. It was still hard to believe Teddy Adler was gone.

And now Liam had made the decision that his grandfather and his mother had been pressing him on—to take over Adler Incorporated, to replace his father. It wasn't the life path Liam wanted, but with his education and background in finance—acquired at the urging of the elder Adler men—he was poised to take over. It was a given. But it didn't fill the gaping hole that his father's death had left behind.

Or the fact that Liam had never wanted to run Adler Inc.

He'd assumed his dad would stay in charge, and then maybe Liam's brothers, Flynn or Ryan, would take over. But even as he thought it, he knew it would never have happened that way. Flynn lived in Los Angeles and was trying to break into acting, and while Ryan resided in Reindeer Pass and had been working for Adler Inc. for the past two years, helping in the real estate division, he didn't have the ambition to run the whole thing. In fact, Ryan was the first to ask Liam to come back.

The bell on the door jingled, and Bella's voice was tight with excitement. "Ellie!"

Ellie Thatcher walked past dressed in a tan wool coat buttoned to a red scarf around her neck and black boots with obvious good traction for the snow-laden sidewalks. She didn't notice him or Ryan, her face split into a giant grin.

"What are you doing here?" Bella asked. "I thought you weren't coming until the end of the week."

"I got my life in order, so I came early," Ellie said, removing red earmuffs and tucking a stray clump of dark hair into the low bun at her nape. "I wanted to surprise you."

When Liam glanced back at his brother, Ryan said quietly, "Looks like I'm not the only one with an eye for a Thatcher girl."

Liam shook his head. "She's the enemy, as is Bella."

Ryan smirked. "That sounds like Gramps talking."

Ellie and Bella continued chatting, with Bella offering a new signature white hot chocolate with eggnog that she'd recently begun serving.

Without comment to Ryan, Liam stood and went to the counter. "I'll take one, too," he said.

Ellie's eyes widened, her cheeks still flush from the cold. "Liam?"

"Hi, Thatcher. It's nice to see you again."

While the stubborn child she'd been was still present in the flash of her eyes, there was something else … a curiosity, a maturity … that tugged at him. Five years ago, she'd been beautiful, but she had been on the cusp of womanhood. The Ellie before him was more fully formed, and he found her more compelling than he would've imagined.

"I didn't know you were back in town," she said, and then her gaze became serious. "I'm sorry about your father. I sent flowers to your mom but signed my name as E. so it wouldn't offend your grandfather."

"Thank you. I'm sure she was appreciative."

"Are you here for the holidays?" she asked.

"Actually, I'm here for good. And you?"

"Also back." She smiled. "For good."

"The family's surprised," Bella said. "You were so determined to see the world."

He let himself indulge a long look, then said, "You'll have to tell me about it some time."

Ellie nodded, and Liam wasn't sure if she was agreeing or simply placating him.

Honking diverted their attention to the street. As people outside moved past the window in a hurried manner, he, Ryan, Ellie, and Bella walked over to see what was happening.

ELLIE'S THROAT constricted as she watched the herd of reindeer moving down the street. As a child, she'd been enamored of the animals, and she'd even finagled her way into working for the Adler Reindeer Farm for nearly two years, only quitting when she'd left for art school in New York City.

Liam Adler stood beside her, and memories of their past encounters—dulled by time and distance—came suddenly into sharp focus.

When she had been ten years old, Liam volunteered to chaperone her into the mountains around Reindeer Pass. She'd been keen to ride a four-wheeler into the backcountry to search for the mythical Arctic reindeer whispered in family lore to have existed.

Three years later, he and Jennifer Dixon, an out-of-town girl he'd been romancing at the time, had intruded on Ellie's forest hideout where she had established a secret lookout to again search for the white reindeer. Jennifer had fallen into a tree well, forcing Ellie to reveal herself and save the poor girl. Ellie had remained in touch intermittently with Jen over the years, but as far as she knew, Jennifer and Liam's relationship had never gone far.

Then, at sixteen, Ellie had gotten a job at the Adler Reindeer Farm with the help of Liam's mother and the begrudging acceptance of her own parents. Everyone had kept Ellie's employment status from the grandfathers. Adam Thatcher and Theo Adler's animosity was well-known, and neither would've approved of Ellie defecting to the enemy camp, but working with the reindeer had been a dream come true for her, and it hadn't hurt that she'd proved to Liam that she had the tenacity to do something he'd said she never could—work for his family.

The last time she'd seen Liam had been the inaugural Reindeer Ball organized by his mother. Five years ago? Had it been that long? She had two distinct memories from that night: Liam's grandfather ordering Liam away from her, and the way Liam had looked at her, as if she were no longer a child.

As that memory surfaced, she became acutely aware of Liam's presence. He was older, his boyishly handsome face having changed to that of a man. She shook off the momentary excitement of seeing him again, but he and reindeer had always been linked for her, so it was yet another odd coincidence that a random wild herd was suddenly making their way through the slushy streets of Barstow.

Bella shaded her eyes. "Are those Adler reindeer?" she asked.

"No." Ellie and Liam answered at the same time.

She caught his gaze. "I worked at the farm, remember?" Then she said to Bella, "The Adlers mark the ears of their herd with a notch. These are wild but probably go back to that original herd our families had imported in the 1800's." She watched the animals tromping by with a bit of awe—ten in all, several sporting large antlers. That would make them female since the males would have shed theirs by now.

Ellie pulled her cellphone from her coat pocket and began snapping photos. "Have they done this before?" she asked, wishing she had one of her cameras, but her gear was back at the Thatcher house in Reindeer Pass with the rest of her luggage.

"No," Bella said. "I've had the bakery for two years and have never seen this. Does your family want to capture them?" she asked Ryan.

Ryan shrugged. "Nah. We have enough at the farm, but I didn't realize there were wild herds, or that they'd come this far down the mountain."

The reindeer headed toward a creek at the edge of Barstow.

Excitement coursed through Ellie. After bouncing across Europe on various photography assignments, she'd spent the last year and a half in Finland, developing an affinity for the place that was surely tied to her Finnish ancestry, despite that her grandfather always spoke about their British Thatcher roots.

She was struck by how similar Reindeer Pass and Barstow were to Finland. Her great-great grandmother, Eleonoora Korhonen Thatcher, for whom she was named, had come to Reindeer Pass sometime in the 1890's from Finland with her father to deliver a reindeer herd to Charlie Thatcher and Henry Adler. She'd stayed when she'd fallen in love with Charlie and married him.

So Ellie had embraced her Finnish heritage, learning the language and spending as much time as she could in Lapland, the northernmost part of the country. And of course, getting to know the local reindeer. But then her mother had had a medical scare—breast nodules that had ultimately turned out to be benign—but it had shaken Ellie, stirring a homesickness that became difficult to ignore. It had been time to come home.

"If these are wild, then …." she said half to herself.

"I can guess what you're thinking," Liam said.

She glanced at him, his blue eyes causing a nervous tumble in her stomach. It was just Liam Adler. No reason to get all flustered.

"And what's that?" she asked.

"That if there are wild reindeer then the Vaadin must be real."

As a girl, she'd been obsessed with finding the Arctic reindeer that might or might not live in the mountains around here, and old Eustace Hapgood, who lived in a remote cabin in the hills, had told her and Liam about the legend of the Vaadin, a magnificent and rare female Arctic reindeer. To see her was to be blessed with true love. Or something like that. But Ellie had learned during her extended stay in Finland the Vaadin was more of a divine ancestor to the mountain reindeer, a goddess who could forge magical artifacts.

"You remember that?" she asked. "Do you know if Eustace is still alive?"

"Are you talking about Eustace Hapgood?" Ryan asked.

She nodded.

"He's still around," Ryan said. "There's talk he wants to sell his property. Adler Inc. is interested, but he's rebuffed our efforts to talk about it."

Ellie wondered if her grandfather would want to buy the Hapgood property, since the Adlers already owned much of the mountain. When Grandpa Adam and Liam's grandfather had feuded over a woman—Ellie's grandmother—Grandpa Adam had given his share of the reindeer they had imported from Finland to Mr. Adler. When Ellie was younger, she had thought it not fair. She had so wanted her family to have access to the amazing animals. If the Adlers bought Eustace's property, would it also include the Arctic reindeer that could be living in the mountains?

"And that Vaadin thing you mentioned has changed things," Ryan added.

"How's that?" Ellie asked.

"You've missed all the hoopla by being away," Bella interjected. "The Vaadin is our Loch Ness Monster."

Ryan buttoned his wool coat. "The myth of the Vaadin has grown into big business around here."

"How did I miss all of this?" Liam asked. "I guess I haven't been paying attention."

"It's called the Christmas Village." Ryan nodded toward the mountain visible beyond town. "It's off the bypass road that leads to Eustace's place."

"People come from all over to try and find it," Bella said. "The gift shops have the creature on everything from t-shirts to mugs to magnets. It's a bit overdone but good for business."

"Who started it?" Ellie asked, finding it hard to believe it was Eustace. The man had spoken reverently of the myth of the Vaadin, and he had seemed to value his privacy.

Bella rubbed her hands together and blew on them. "Mark Osborn. He brought in some marketing people and has been expanding it ever since."

"Unbelievable," Ellie muttered, a surge of irritation flashing through her that Mark would take advantage of Eustace and the reindeer lore of this area. "Maybe whoever buys Eustace's land could shut it all down."

Bella shrugged. "The Christmas Village isn't on his land, but I'm sure Mark is itching to purchase it as well. It would make it easy for him to grow."

The wild reindeer were now out of sight, so Ellie checked her watch.

"Bells, I have an appointment," she said. "But I'll stop by later."

"I close at five. We can go to dinner at the Bistro."

"Sounds good." Ellie shifted her attention between Ryan and Liam, trying to give them equal time, but even when she didn't look at Liam, she was all too aware of him. "Nice to see you both."

"I have to leave as well," Liam said.

"You're going to take care of that appointment for me?" Ryan asked his brother.

"Yep."

Liam started walking in the same direction as Ellie, and they moved side by side in an awkward silence.

She tucked her phone into her coat pocket. "You're not following me, are you?"

"Maybe you're following me."

When she spied her destination from the address the realtor had emailed her, she reached for the door handle, and Liam's gloved hand brushed hers, startling her.

"What …?" she said.

"You're going here?" He spoke at the same time.

She nodded, a little too vigorously, but he didn't seem to notice. Instead, he pushed open the door and waited for her to precede him. As they entered the empty store—a bit musty with random furniture strewn about—she stopped short when the realtor turned to face them.

Mark Osborn smiled, then looked shocked, then disgusted. "You're the clients?" he asked. He hadn't changed much over the years, he was still stocky, but his normally gel-filled curly hair was instead cut short. The last time she'd seen Mark had been the same night she'd last been with Liam.

"Hi, Mark," Ellie said reluctantly. "Where's Tammy?" she asked, referring to the woman she'd been corresponding with.

"She had a family emergency," he said. "Her kid swallowed a quarter."

"That's terrible," Ellie said. "I hope he's okay."

Mark's gaze flicked between Ellie and Liam, who had been quiet so far. "Tammy said I was meeting with a Thatcher and an Adler, but I thought it was your angry grandfathers. Are you both still together?"

"Oh." Ellie frowned. "No."

But when Mark's expression appeared a bit intrigued, Ellie regretted denying it. Liam had not only pretended to be her date but also her boyfriend to get Mark off her back. Osborn had been aggressively pursuing her after a few platonic dates and wouldn't take no for an answer. When Liam had stepped in, Ellie had been relieved. And then slightly confused because her reaction to Liam had been decidedly different than to Mark.

Liam focused on her, ignoring Mark. "Why are you looking at this property?" he asked.

"I'm planning to open a photography studio."

He nodded, a slight smile tugging at his mouth, and she couldn't help but feel that he was somehow pleased by her answer.

"And you?" she asked.

"I'm taking over Adler Inc. Gramps wants to lease a bigger office in Barstow than the one Ryan currently works at."

"Would this be large enough for you?" She gestured to the small storefront.

Liam hesitated, then said in a quiet voice, "He wants the entire building."

Mark glanced at his notes. "The entire building? Oh yes, it's here." He lifted his gaze to her. "It'll be tough for you to match that offer, Ellie."

She bristled at Osborn's smug tone, but he was right. She took in the quaint wooden counter, the high ceiling that would allow for ample wall space for photos from her travels, and the fantastic morning light spilling through the front windows. Not to mention that she'd be down the street from Bella.

She couldn't afford the lease, of course, but Grandpa Thatcher had set up this meeting, telling her he would invest in her future. Did he know that Theo Adler also wanted the space? Did she want to be the cause of stoking their feud even further?

Mark chuckled. "Well, who's going to butter me up the most?"

Ellie's shoulders sagged.

Liam kept his attention on her. "I'll talk to Gramps," he said. "We'll look for another building."

"You will?" she asked.

With a nod, he said, "You should take it, Thatcher."

Surprised by his gesture, she said, "Thank you."

Liam turned to Mark. "Make sure she gets a good deal. And tell Tammy that Adler Inc. will need to see other properties."

"Will do," Mark said, then he looked at Ellie with a gleam in his eyes. "Let's go back to the office to sign the papers."

The last thing Ellie wanted was to spend the next hour with Mark Osborn, and she had an irrational wish that Liam would accompany them.

She gave a silent acknowledgement to Mark, then said, "Thanks again, Liam."

He smiled. "See you around."

She tried not to stare as he stepped onto the sidewalk and closed the door behind him.

Two

Two weeks later, Ellie hung the last photograph on the wall of her new studio. It was a shot of an hours-old reindeer calf from her time in Lapland. The newborn female had been all legs and gawkiness, and it was one of her favorite photos. And it had been especially nice when it had graced the cover of a local Finnish nature magazine.

She stood back and took in the space she'd been working diligently on for her new business.

Most of the photos were from her time in Finland, but she'd also had the opportunity to visit the Dolomites in Italy, the mountain town of Chamonix in France, and the Ring of Brodgar in the Orkney Islands, so she'd included them as well.

The floors were cleaned and buffed, and the countertops decorated with poinsettia plants, evergreen sprigs, pinecones, and colorful holiday Christmas ball ornaments, although all the flora was fake since she anticipated having children on the premises for photoshoots. In that vein, she had an album with pictures she'd taken of people ready to show potential customers. Her hope was to work with locals on family portraits, weddings, and kids' photos, but she was open to commercial jobs as well. Probably not the best time to start a business with Christmas right around the corner, but it would give her a chance to get settled before work hopefully picked up after the new year. It was Friday, and with the hard labor done, she'd spend the weekend working on her website in preparation for her opening on Monday.

In the meantime, she had an offer from Hilltop Magazine. An editor she'd worked with had been interested in the history of the Thatcher and Adler families and their ties to the local reindeer herds, and when Ellie had mentioned the myth of the Vaadin, the editor had liked it even more. She'd asked Ellie to piece together an article, not only taking photos, but also writing the story, which she had sometimes done in the past. At least it would help with the bills since her savings wouldn't last forever, and she didn't plan on leaning on her grandfather indefinitely. For now he was paying the rent and utilities, for which she was grateful.

Now that she'd been in both Barstow and Reindeer Pass for a few weeks, she'd had the chance to visit the souvenir shops and tourist hangouts in both towns, and the Vaadin was a bit of a local celebrity. The Osborn marketing strategy had done its job. There had been the poster hanging in Mark's office at the realty company, a rendering of a mystical creature set against a backdrop of sparkly snow that was far from what an average Arctic reindeer might look like. Shops sold Vaadin figurines, tea towels, and sweatshirts with the creature's supposed likeness, and chocolate bars wrapped in reindeer magic. Tours to the Christmas Village hinted at the possibility of being the first to find the creature in real life, but a photo with an actual reindeer *was* guaranteed. Ellie learned that Mark had rented two animals from the Adler Reindeer Farm and was keeping them in the Village for the winter.

As much as Ellie was loath to admit, a part of her wanted to visit the place.

It all sounded so downright enchanting.

But she was trying to take the high ground, since Eustace's property abutted Osborn land and she couldn't help but feel that Mark was exploiting the old man. According to Ellie's father, Mark was trying to buy Eustace's land, should the property go up for sale, and so were her grandfather and Liam's grandfather as well. Eustace's land was surrounded by Osborn, Adler, and Thatcher land, making it highly coveted by all three parties.

But as yet Eustace hadn't moved forward with a listing, so everyone was in waiting mode.

Thinking of the Vaadin and reindeer stories and everyone acting like buying land was some kind of chess game had helped with one thing—keeping her mind off Liam Adler.

She hadn't seen him since that day when she'd run into him in Bella's bakery. A bit of covert questioning had turned up that he was indeed back to stay, and he was single. Not that it made a difference. Thatchers couldn't date Adlers. Why would they want to? Adlers were nothing but trouble.

The bell on the door jingled as her grandfather entered.

"Hi, Grandpa."

"How's my girl doing?" He grinned wide, his gray beard and mustache cropped close.

"Everything's going well." She indicated the space with

a sweep of her arm. "Thank you again for helping me get started."

He removed his gloves but kept his thick jacket buttoned. "It's nice to have you back, sweetheart, and this was a small price to pay for it."

Her attention was captured by two men outside the storefront. The first was easily recognizable—Liam. Her heartrate jumped at the sight of him, and she grimaced. *No need for that, Ellie.* The other man, almost as tall as Liam, was Theo Adler, Liam's grandfather. And if she hadn't been sure it were him, then his both appalled and surprised reaction to the writing on the window—ELLIE THATCHER PHOTOGRAPHY—tipped her off. Mr. Adler pushed open the door and came inside like a bull ready for a head butt, Liam talking rapidly to the man who was steadfastly ignoring his grandson.

Ellie took a breath, bracing herself. Before she could warn Grandpa Adam about what was coming, he turned and faced the horns bearing down on him.

"What the hell is going on here?" Theo Adler demanded, his receding hairline revealing a shiny forehead.

"Gramps, I can explain," Liam said, glancing her way with a look of apology in his eyes.

Great. Somehow, she was in the middle of this.

"Is this your shop?" the elder Mr. Adler demanded of her.

"Y-yes." Worry gripped her. What had she done?

Mr. Adler shifted his attention to her grandfather. "Was this your doing, Adam?"

Grandpa Adam squared off against his nemesis. "If you mean helping my granddaughter realize her dream of running her own studio, then yes."

"Well, you both need to leave. I own this building and I

sure as hell never gave you a lease. Don't make me sue you."

"Gramps," Liam cut in, "calm down. They do have a lease."

Mr. Adler frowned at his grandson. "What are you talking about?"

"I didn't sign a contract with Adler Inc.," Ellie said, alarmed by the turn of events. "It was with Ludlow and Sons." What was supposed to be a fun day of putting the finishing touches on the studio had quickly gone south.

Liam looked at her. "Gramps wasn't trying to lease the building as I'd thought. He was buying it and the deal closed two days ago. I told Mark Osborn we would honor the existing leases." He pulled an envelope from his jacket pocket. "In fact, I was on my way here to explain everything and have you sign a new contract."

"I didn't approve that, Liam," Mr. Adler growled.

Liam faced his grandfather. "Yes, you did. We discussed an already existing tenant on the ground floor. You agreed they could stay."

"I didn't realize it was a Thatcher. I rescind the agreement."

Ellie was about to speak, but Grandpa Adam stepped forward. "You're really going to kick out my granddaughter? I'll sue *you*."

The two of them began arguing and Ellie glared at Liam.

"Enough," Liam said in a stern voice. "Gramps, you gave me free rein to run the company, and yet you neglected to tell me about this purchase, so I'm honoring the lease. Ellie's business is a good addition to Main Street." Then Liam met her gaze. "Unless you want to leave. You can, of course, break the existing contract, and we won't penalize you for it."

"Why are you being so soft on a Thatcher, Liam?" his grandfather huffed.

"Look, I don't profess to understand all the reasons for the animosity the two of you have," Liam said, "but how about showing some common human decency? Ellie's done a nice job with the interior. I'm not about to make her start over somewhere else."

Grandpa Adam turned to her. "Do you want to stay?"

While it didn't seem worth the additional family strife, she was in love with the space. She nodded, her voice resolute as she said, "Yes."

Her grandfather turned back to Mr. Adler. "Then I expect you not to harass my granddaughter."

Theo Adler leaned close. "That goes both ways." Then he left the store, barking over his shoulder, "Don't be late for supper, Liam."

A charged silence ensued in his wake.

Ellie finally spoke. "Why can't the two of you get along?"

A resigned and half-hearted smile tugged at her grandfather's lips. "I've tried. He's so goddamned stubborn. But then so am I."

"It must've been hard for him when Grandma chose you over him."

Her grandfather again nodded, his demeanor contemplative, but he didn't elaborate. Instead, he reached for the envelope Liam held. "Let me have a look at that. Can't have you taking advantage of Ellie."

"I'd never do that, sir," Liam said.

An hour later, they had ironed out the details of the lease—Grandpa Adam had argued over the late fee and the terms for eviction and Liam had compromised on both. She signed, and her grandfather had left.

"World War III averted," she said when they were both alone.

"Barely. Listen, I'm sorry about all that. I only just learned about it. There's been a mountain of work to get through since my father died. My grandfather likes to think he's still on top of it all, but the truth is he's let a lot of things slide."

She accepted his answer, quelling her annoyance over the argument between their grandfathers. For a moment she'd thought all her hard work these past two weeks was going to be for naught. Unfortunately, she needed something else from an Adler, and she'd much rather ask Liam than Theo Adler.

"I was wondering if I could ask for a favor," she said. "I have a magazine assignment involving reindeer in the area. I'll be going into the mountains to photograph the wild herds, but I doubt they'll saunter down Main Street again like they did the other day. All I had were my cellphone photos for that one." She made sure she always had her Canon on her now, along with a long lens.

"I might cross onto Adler land," she continued. "And I wonder if I could have permission to do so. Also, could I come to the farm and photograph the Adler domestic herds?"

Liam hesitated. "I'm happy to say yes, but as you can see my grandfather is a different story. I don't think it's wise keeping this from him. How about you come for dinner tonight and you can ask him yourself?"

She laughed. "I could've asked him an hour ago right here, but as you saw he doesn't exactly like me. I was kinda hoping to avoid him from here on out."

"I never pegged you for a chicken, Thatcher."

Ellie suppressed a grumble at his goading.

"I'll tell you what," he said. "Why don't you bring Bella. That way you won't be like a deer among wolves."

"You're all wolves?"

"My mother will be there, and she does like you, so you'd have that."

"And what about you, Liam? Do you like me?" Too late, she couldn't take it back. It sounded like she was fishing for a compliment, and a hot flush crept up her cheeks.

"I've never liked you, Thatcher." But the heat in his eyes said otherwise. Then it was over, and he was walking to the door. "I'll text you the address."

"It's all right," she said. "I know the location of the Adler Mansion."

"Be there around six for cocktails."

He left her shop, and she didn't know what to think. He'd made it sound like a date. Had she imagined the wanting that had escaped his eyes before he'd tamped it down?

Her heart pounded.

Should she go? Did she have a choice? In the wilderness, she wasn't certain she would know the property lines. And with the way her luck was running, she'd end up on Adler land, shoot a fantastic photo, it would be published, and then Theo Adler would see it and sue her, claiming she'd been trespassing on his property.

No. She would like this to be on the up and up.

She finished cleaning while she wondered what she should wear to an Adler family dinner.

Three

When the knock came at the front door, Liam made sure he got there first.

On the other side was Ellie, wearing a maroon wool coat, her dark hair spilling over her shoulders. She looked a bit stressed but otherwise confident. He'd always liked that about her. She'd had a natural courage as a girl, and he was glad to see she hadn't lost it. Bella stood beside her, her back straight beneath a matching white hat, scarf, and mittens that contrasted her dark hair. There didn't seem to be any blondes on the Thatcher side.

"Please come in," he said, stepping back as they entered the foyer.

"I brought a chocolate peppermint cake," Bella said, indicating the item she carried wrapped in cellophane and topped with a big red bow.

Liam took it from her. "Thank you."

While the girls shed their winter gear, Liam texted his brother that Bella was here for dinner, guessing that Ryan wouldn't want to miss this. He should have mentioned it earlier, but he wasn't sure if Ellie would bring her cousin. Or if Ellie would show at all.

His brother replied almost immediately, putting the emoji of an exploding head beside *gramps* and then followed with, *I'll be right there. Just closing up the office now.*

They needed to move Adler Inc. to the new building in Barstow—the one that Ellie now occupied on the bottom floor—and Ryan had started to box up files and supplies after hours.

Liam led the girls into the spacious sitting room as his grandmother, Charlotte, joined them. Liam had already told her that Ellie might be coming by so she could be prepared, and she had surprised him by smiling, clearly delighted by the prospect.

"Ellie, welcome," his grandmother beamed, her silver bob tucked behind her ears. "Bella, you came too." She gave each girl a hug. "It's a shame it's taken this long to have you both over."

The wrinkle on Ellie's forehead conveyed her bewilderment, matching Liam's. He'd had no idea his grandmother had been waiting to have a Thatcher over for dinner.

Liam's mother breezed into the room, dressed casually in jeans and a green sweater, her blonde hair pinned back and some color in her cheeks. He was glad to see her in a somewhat cheerful mood. The grief had been hitting her especially hard this week.

"It's so nice for you both to join us," she said. And then to Ellie, "You were one of our best employees at the reindeer farm."

"It was one of my favorite jobs. I'm so sorry about Mr. Adler."

"Thank you."

Guilt hit him again. His mother had said that having

him close was helping, which made him feel badly that he wasn't as excited as he should be to take over the day-to-day management of Adler Inc. It was one reason he was still letting Ryan handle most of the daily issues, while he tried to understand the bigger picture of all the holdings his grandfather had amassed over the years. With hope, it would get better in time.

As Ellie and Bella chatted with his mother and grandmother, it was clear the Adler and Thatcher women didn't seem to hold a grudge like the grandfathers did. But it was also true that they didn't seek out the other's company, always remaining a respectful distance. Except when his mother had been behind hiring a teenaged Ellie to work at the farm. The move had surprised Liam when he'd learned of it, but his mother had remarked at the time that *Ellie has a light in her eyes around the reindeer, and they respond to her.*

How had he not seen how sentimental his mother was about the animals? And judging by the way she was talking to Ellie, about Ellie herself.

"We don't want to impose," Ellie was saying when his mother insisted she and Bella stay for dinner. "I just need to speak with the older Mr. Adler."

"You're a brave one, I'll give you that." His mother squeezed Ellie's arm and smiled. "He's not here yet, so let's have a drink and we'll set two extra places at the table."

"Ryan is on his way," Liam said, and Bella seemed to briefly perk up over that news. "What can I get you both?"

"Sparkling water?" Ellie asked.

"I'll have the same," Bella added.

Liam nodded, pouring the drinks over glasses of ice and adding a slice of lemon. As everyone sat, Ryan entered and if the redness on his cheeks was any indication, he'd run the entire way. Liam suppressed a smirk.

"Sorry I'm late," his brother said.

"Hi, Ryan," Ellie said, and Bella offered a smile.

Ryan was about to say more when Gramps arrived, kicking snow off his boots and removing them before he entered the roomful of women staring at him. Belatedly, Liam realized he was staring too, the tension in the room suddenly thick.

"We have guests, Gramps," Liam said.

"I can see that." He ran a hand over his thinning hair.

Charlotte came to her husband and kissed his cheek, murmuring softly to him. He gave a slight nod of acknowledgement.

"Girls," he said to Ellie and Bella.

Ellie stood and cleared her throat. "Hello, Mr. Adler." She reached out a hand. "Thank you for allowing me into your home."

Gramps squinted and then relented, shaking her hand. "You've got gumption, I'll give you that."

Liam relaxed just a hair. Maybe this evening wouldn't be a total disaster.

"Thank you, sir. There's a reason I've come. That *we've* come." She indicated Bella who was still sitting on the sofa looking very uncomfortable.

When Gramps didn't respond, Ellie quickly continued. "You see," she said, clearing her throat once again. "I've been given a magazine assignment to photograph the wild reindeer in these mountains, and I'm planning on looking for them and should I happen to stumble, well … although I'll try not to, I might accidentally cross the wrong property line."

When she paused for a breath, Gramps said in a calm voice, "Spit it out, dear."

"Can I go onto your land?"

A prickly silence descended on the room.

Gramps finally shook his head and sighed. "I suppose you'll go anyway."

"Not on purpose, sir. I did go into the hills frequently when I was a child, and I'm afraid I didn't always pay attention to where I was. I asked Liam"—she glanced at him—"but he said I needed to speak with you."

Gramps cast a censuring look at Liam. "You keep her shop from me, but not this?" He raised an eyebrow.

"What's this about Ellie's shop?" his mother asked.

"Liam has leased the first floor to her in that building I just bought in Barstow," Gramps said, but he didn't seem as angry as he'd been earlier.

His mother cast a surprised look his way.

"I didn't realize it was an Adler building," Ellie said to his mother. "Liam didn't tell me until today."

"It didn't seem right to break the lease just because she was a Thatcher," Liam said quietly.

His mother's expression softened before turning to her father-in-law. "I'm sure it will be fine, Theo." Then to Ellie, she said, "What kind of shop are you opening?"

"A photography studio."

"That's wonderful. I'll have to stop by."

"That would be lovely, Mrs. Adler. I'm planning to open on Monday."

"Look," Gramps said, raising his voice. "I'm not terribly keen on you wandering around Adler land unchaperoned. God knows we have enough problems with all those tourists looking for some damned mythical reindeer. Speaking of which, Liam, that's our first order of business."

"What's that?"

"Dealing with Osborn and his Christmas machine up there on the mountain, along with Hapgood. If he's selling the land, then we need to buy it, so you'll go up there with her and deal with it all at once, since you're such a Thatcher sympathizer and all."

"I can assure you that I'll be careful," Ellie said. "I've been in the field the last three years. I have experience in the mountains, especially in northern Finland. I don't need a chaperone."

"Well, that might be the case," Gramps said. "But you'll not be out there alone. You shouldn't have done it when you were a child, but that's a moot point now. You could've gotten hurt or worse. I'll not be responsible for that, and God knows that Adam would drag me to court over it."

Liam frowned. He hadn't realized how much Theo and Adam threatened litigation with one another.

"Liam, you'll go with her."

While spending the day with Ellie Thatcher wouldn't be a hardship, he knew he couldn't keep putting off Adler Inc. business. "Ryan handles the real estate side. Let him talk to Eustace, as well as Osborn."

"Eustace won't talk to me," Ryan said from across the room. "And you're the boss now, Liam. You should check out what Osborn has going on up there. You're the one who gets to decide what to do."

Liam wasn't so sure of that. While he was technically in charge, Gramps' fingerprints were still all over everything, and his opinion could be heard from miles away. Liam wasn't under any illusion that he was the final word, as was clearly in play with him ordering Liam to babysit Ellie.

"It's all right, sir," Ellie cut in. "I'll be fine out there. I promise my grandfather won't sue you."

"That's a sweet sentiment, young lady, but that's not a promise you can make. Besides, I know that Adam is after Hapgood's land too. So how do I know you're not going to undermine the deal somehow on his behalf?"

She shook her head, looking perplexed. "I'm not. I can assure you I'm not involved at all."

"Nevertheless, Liam you'll keep an eye on her."

Ellie glared in his direction, frustration written all over her face.

"Dinner is ready," his mother said, breaking up the standoff.

They all walked into the dining room. Normally, Liam and Ryan sat near Gramps so they could talk business despite his grandmother insisting the supper table was for family and not work, but Liam thought it might be wise to give Gramps some distance from Ellie, or maybe it was the other way around, so he guided their guests to the opposite end of the table, and he and Ryan sat with the girls while his mother and grandmother bookended Gramps.

A cook served plates with salad for everyone.

"It's like you live in a palace," Bella murmured.

Ryan leaned forward. "We've heard the Thatchers dine on crystal plates and drink from gold goblets."

Bella's expression remained serious as she said, "We also ride unicorns."

Ellie laughed. "When did you get a sense of humor, Bells?"

Bella raised her eyebrows and munched on her salad.

"Do you all live here?" Ellie asked Ryan.

"Yeah," Ryan replied, and Liam wondered if Ryan was feeling as embarrassed of that as he was. Except that the house was large, and it had always been nice to be near his folks when he visited. And now … well, he didn't feel comfortable leaving his mom alone.

"Eventually we'll find our own places," Liam said.

Ryan looked at him with a bit of confusion. That had

never been on the table. But it should be. They were grown men. He didn't examine too closely why he cared what Ellie thought, but surely if Ryan were hoping for any type of romance with Bella, then he had to know it couldn't possibly happen while living under this roof.

"I'm with my parents for now, but after the new year I'm going to look for something too," Ellie said.

The rest of the evening was uneventful, and Gramps behaved himself at the first Adler and Thatcher dinner. After Ellie and Bella said their goodbyes and left, his mother faced both him and Ryan.

"They're nice girls," she said, a rare gleam in her eye. "Goodnight, boys."

Gramps sighed from his chair in front of the fireplace, his nightly glass of whiskey in hand. "I suppose they are. For Thatchers."

Bright and early on Saturday morning, Ellie stood on the sidewalk in front of her studio, bouncing on her heels from the biting cold. Liam had texted her last night that he'd drive her up the mountain, and she had suggested meeting here since the road was more accessible from the Barstow side rather than from Reindeer Pass. Plus, having him pick her up at her parents' house where she was currently staying just seemed unnecessary. Too many questions to answer. She'd deal with it later, as she was sure that word of her and Liam in the wilderness would get out soon enough.

An SUV with two snowmobiles on a trailer pulled up, Liam behind the wheel. He left it idling as he stepped out and came to the sidewalk.

"Where did you get those?" she asked.

"Good morning to you, too." He wore a dark green fleece and a black knit hat. "I thought these might make it easier to get into the backcountry more quickly. I know you aren't thrilled to have me tag along, and I'm not thrilled to be a babysitter."

"It's not that I don't want you along, it's just that I'd been hoping for a bit of solitude. And hiking would be quieter."

"Making a pilgrimage, are you?"

"Something like that."

He opened the passenger door and she climbed in, stashing her backpack at her feet, but Liam took it from her. "Be careful with that," she added. "It has all my camera equipment."

He nodded and put it on the bench seat behind her. He came back to the driver's side, hopped in, then guided the land rover onto the icy streets. It was early so there was little traffic. He stopped in front of Bella's Bakery.

To her questioning look, he said, "Sustenance."

Ellie thought about remaining in the car since she hadn't told Bella that she and Liam had made plans. In Bella's mind, the whole business about Ellie going into the mountains was just talk and she'd said after their dinner at the Adlers that Ellie should remain on Thatcher land and that would be that.

Ellie hadn't really shared the entirety of her plans to photograph the reindeer with anyone in the family. They would tell her she was still chasing her childhood fascination with the creatures, and truthfully, maybe they were right. But she wanted to go, nevertheless.

How strange that Liam Adler was by her side once again, as he'd always seemed to be when they were kids.

As she and Liam entered the bakery, Bella greeted them with a surprised look on her face. "You two aren't wasting any time," she said.

Ellie shrugged, pulling off her winter mittens. "Can we order? Or is it too early?"

"Depends on what you want."

"How about a London Fog and a blueberry muffin," Ellie said.

Liam scanned the menu on the wall. "I'll have a black coffee and a breakfast sandwich."

"I can do that." Bella rang up the order and Liam paid.

While they waited Ellie noticed a flyer on the counter.

MEET THE VAADIN AND SANTA CLAUS

"It's Eustace."

Liam took the advertisement from her and scanned it. "Osborn must be behind this."

"How did he convince Eustace to do it? It seems so … commercial."

"Maybe we should stop in and visit him."

Ellie nodded, tucking the flyer into her coat pocket.

Bella delivered their order, and Ellie waved bye as she and Liam resumed their journey. The muffin was warm and melted in her mouth, the tea hot and creamy, and the scenery amazing as they climbed out of the valley and into the mountains. Sunlight illuminated the forest, causing the freshly fallen snow to sparkle with a thousand tiny crystals. A happy, fuzzy emotion settled in her stomach, and being in Liam's company felt like the most natural place for her to be in the world.

"I checked out your website," he said.

"Really? I just finished it last night."

"It looks good. You've been busy these past few years. I just can't figure out why you came back."

"I missed it."

"Missed what?"

"This place. Reindeer Pass. My family. Don't get me wrong, it was fun to travel, and I especially enjoyed my time in Finland, but nothing beats home." She sipped her earl grey tea. Bella had done a nice job of blending the added cream with a hint of vanilla.

"And you don't have any doubts about returning?"

"No." She ate the last of her muffin. "Do you?"

"I never planned to return."

"Never ever?"

"Well, to visit, of course. But when I left, I thought that was it."

She got more comfortable in her seat and watched his profile as he effortlessly guided the vehicle along the winding turns. "Haven't you been groomed for years as the heir apparent to the Adler fortune?"

He gave a cynical laugh. "It's not quite a fortune. And I suppose Gramps saw me in charge one day, but I really thought my dad would be around for a lot longer." His voice trailed off, his distress obvious.

"Some things we can't account for," she murmured, a pang of sympathy for him. "The whims of fate and all that. What about Ryan? Or Flynn? Couldn't they take over so you can live far away from your family, alone and lonely?"

Liam cast an annoyed look at her. "You're not a very supportive passenger."

She drained the last of her tea and said, "I think you're wrong, Liam. What could be more important than family. And our families have such history here. Don't you want to be a part of that?"

"You want to live in a town where our grandfathers actively hate each other?"

"I think it's only a problem if our grandfathers hate *us*."

His brows crashed together, and he looked appalled.

She laughed. "So serious, Adler."

"Somebody has to be with all you free spirits running around."

That made her laugh harder.

"What if we're here for a reason?" she asked.

"And now we're getting back to fate."

She didn't feel like sharing the deep pull that had prompted her to return, beginning with worry over her mom but also woven together with reindeer and home and probably Liam himself. Shaking off that foolish notion, she said instead, "What if we could heal the rift between our families?"

"As long as you pick something easy."

"Chicken."

A large sign appeared: CHRISTMAS VILLAGE UP AHEAD.

"Shall we stop?" Liam asked, ignoring her jab.

"May as well," she replied, feigning a nonchalance she wasn't feeling. She was excited to see this village.

Since it was still early, only a few cars sat in the parking lot. Liam parked off to the side since he had the trailer behind his SUV. He pulled on his coat and hat while Ellie did the same, and they walked toward the arched entryway with CHRISTMAS VILLAGE written in large wooden letters across it.

A quick inspection showed a café, a ticket booth for cross-country skiing and tubing, a gazebo with a big wooden chair presumably for Santa, and off to the side was an oversized fake Arctic reindeer, a big sign proclaiming a photo-op with the Vaadin.

"Wow." Ellie was turning in a circle, clear delight on her face. It reminded him of young Ellie, exasperating and stubborn and filled with a passion for these mountains that for some reason had always made him feel … happy.

She pointed at a pen occupied by two real reindeer with large racks. "Those are from the Adler Farm."

"It looks like it. The reindeer get rented out for various events in the winter."

She went to the fence and reached out a hand. "Hi, girls." One of them came to Ellie and snuffled against her palm. "I know you. You're Ruby. You remember me."

Liam didn't know the reindeer at the Adler Farm by name. In fact, he hardly interacted with them and certainly wouldn't have recognized one outside of the business.

Both animals were now vying for Ellie's attention, and she was showering love over them.

"Ellie?" a woman's voice said excitedly from behind them.

Liam recognized her immediately. Jennifer Dixon. Years ago, they'd gone on a few dates. There'd even been the incident in the woods when she'd fallen into a tree well and a teenaged Ellie had helped to rescue her. Not really his proudest moment when he'd briefly panicked, recalling his own headfirst incident when he was a boy. But Ellie had kept her cool and had managed the rescue with a calm demeanor.

The two women hugged.

"I had no idea you were back," Jennifer was saying, then her attention shifted to him, and her smile slipped a notch. "Liam. What a surprise."

"Hi, Jennifer. Nice to see you."

"Are you both back in town?"

"Yes," Ellie answered. "For good. Both of us."

"I heard about your father, Liam. I'm so sorry. You've come back to run the family business?"

"I have."

"Well, I see you both found the Adler reindeer." Jennifer smiled, looking professional in her full-length wool coat and fur-lined snow boots, her blonde hair tucked into an elegant bun.

"Are you involved with this?" Ellie indicated the village. Activity was picking up as employees opened stalls and the café doors were unlocked.

"I am. I was working in marketing in Denver, but two years ago Mark Osborn offered me a job with his development company. We came up with this together."

"Impressive," Liam said.

"So you live in Barstow now?" Ellie asked.

"I do. My parents are full-time too. All those holidays spent skiing here really gave me a love for the town and the area. There's so much potential here."

Jennifer caught sight of someone and waved them over. "Mark! Come say hi."

Mark Osborn was walking with none other than Eustace. It had been eight years since Liam had seen him, and he was surprisingly spry for his age, because he'd been an old man even then. His hair was still a shock of white, and his beard was so bushy that he resembled Santa Claus but a good deal skinnier.

Dressed for the office rather than an outdoor park, Mark said, "Do you both know Eustace Hapgood?"

"Yes," Ellie said. "It's good to see you, Mr. Hapgood. You're looking good."

"Thank you, Ellie."

"You remember me."

"I may be old but I'm not senile." He paused. "Not yet, at least."

Eustace shook Liam's hand. "I'm sorry I couldn't come to the funeral, son. I was under the weather. Your father was a good man."

"Thank you."

"Eustace is our Santa Claus," Mark said, placing a hand on the old man's shoulders, a proprietary move that Liam didn't miss.

"You look the part," Ellie said. "But I have to admit I'm surprised by all this emphasis on the Vaadin."

"Do you like it?" Mark asked. "When Eustace told me the stories, I thought it was such a unique angle, so why not bring it to the children in town as well as the tourists. In fact, we're about to open and I need to get Eustace into costume. It ruins the magic if the kids see him out and about."

"Of course," Ellie said. "But might I ask a favor, Eustace?"

Eustace nodded.

"I'm on an assignment to photograph the wild reindeer in the mountains here in Barstow and Reindeer Pass. Would it be okay if I went on your property?"

"They tend to congregate around Eustace's cabin," Mark offered.

"Really?" Ellie said.

"Well, not since Lilja," Eustace said.

"Who's Lilja?" Jennifer asked.

"A dog. She showed up one day and does nothing but bark at the reindeer, so they've been keeping their distance."

"Why do you call her Lilja?" Ellie asked.

"It's Finnish for Lily."

Ellie nodded. "Does she belong to anyone?"

"I called the police and the local shelters, but there's been no report of a missing chocolate lab," he said. "She didn't have a collar. I took her to the vet, and she didn't have one of those chip things. She's a sweet girl, but I'm not going to be able to keep her. Any of you want a dog?" He looked at each of them.

"I would," Ellie said slowly, as if she were surprised by her own answer.

"Excellent," Eustace beamed. "Why don't you stop by later and meet her."

"Okay," Ellie said, glancing at Liam. "What time?"

"I'm here until two o'clock. In fact, why don't all four of you come to my cabin."

Suspicion filled Mark's gaze. "Why?"

"Well, I need to make a decision about my property, and seeing the four of you now has got me thinking."

Suspicion turned to eagerness, and Mark said, "You're going to sell?"

"I am."

"My realty company will be happy to run the listing." The gleam in Mark's eyes bordered on greedy.

Eustace shook his head. "That won't be necessary."

"Why?" Jennifer asked.

"Because I'm going to sell to one of you."

He walked away, leaving the four of them in a stunned silence.

"What just happened?" Ellie asked. "Do you all want to buy it?"

Liam exchanged a look with Jennifer and Mark, and they all answered, "Yes."

Then Liam said to her, "Doesn't your grandfather want it as well?"

"Yes, of course he does."

Mark leaned in closer. "Look, whatever Eustace is cooking up, we can overcome it. We could all make a deal that whoever gets it sells out."

"To you?" Liam said.

"It makes the most sense. Christmas Village shares a

property line with him. And it's the perfect location for ski-in/ski-out condos. The Adlers and the Thatchers would benefit from the extra tourism on their other properties."

"What about me?" Jennifer asked, a frown marring her face.

"Why do you want the property?" Ellie asked her.

"Well, if you must know, I'm looking for a place to call my own."

Ellie's confused expression matched Liam's. While Jennifer may have changed, during the short time Liam had dated her it had been clear she was a girl who liked her amenities. Eustace's cabin was about as remote as they came.

"And your family?" Ellie said to Liam. "What will they do with it?"

"Land is always a good investment."

He could almost see the wheels turning in Ellie's head. She hadn't liked any of their answers.

Five

Ellie stewed about the encounter with Eustace as Liam drove the SUV to an access road near Eustace's Buckley Cabin.

"We don't have to start on Adler land," she said. "In fact, you really don't have to stay out here with me. I'll just buzz over to Thatcher property." She scanned the tree line. She didn't want to admit that she wasn't sure where Thatcher land began.

"What happened to happy Ellie?" Liam stopped the car and shut it off.

"I'm happy," she defended, her tone less than convincing.

Ellie didn't want to be in the middle of a land fight over Eustace's acreage, but she couldn't help but feel that Mark, Jennifer, and even Liam might not have the best interest of the property in mind. So now she *was* in the middle of it. But would her grandfather also exploit the area? Would Theo Adler? Would Liam?

Could *she* buy the land?

But she had no money, at least not much more than

what was in her savings, and she needed that to feed and clothe herself for the foreseeable future, and she was already beholden to her grandfather for the studio.

She followed Liam to the trailer as he pulled out a ramp and positioned it behind one of the snowmobiles.

"Are you upset about the land?" he asked.

"Why would I be upset?"

"You never hid your moods well, Thatcher. Fight for it."

"For what?"

"The land. If you want it so bad, get your grandfather behind it. But be prepared. Gramps will fight too. And apparently Mark and Jennifer. Who knew they were land thirsty too."

"And you?"

Instead of answering, he climbed onto the platform and undid the straps holding one of the vehicles. He started the motor with a loud rev and brought it slowly backwards down the ramp. He parked it to the side and went to the trailer for the second one, which he had on the ground without a hitch.

As he secured the trailer, he said, "Eustace's property is prime real estate since it would extend either the Adler or Thatcher holdings, and apparently the Osborns. It would be stupid to let an opportunity to buy it pass by."

She couldn't refute his logic.

She tightened the pack on her shoulders then took the helmet Liam offered.

"Do you know how to drive one?" he asked.

"Yes," she said as she pulled the helmet on. "Don't you remember I drove you off the mountain five years ago?" Because he'd had a bit of whiskey courtesy of Eustace.

"That vehicle was older," he said. "These work a little differently. Forward is the same. Just press the throttle with your thumb and release it to stop. These can now go backwards. Let the engine idle and push that yellow reverse button for one second. It will automatically reduce the RPM's and start the engine in a reverse rotation. To return to forward momentum, do the same thing. And always be aware of your surroundings."

She climbed aboard the machine and gave a thumbs up. "Got it. I'll follow you."

They cruised through the woods on a semblance of a path, since they'd started from a side road, but soon enough they were breaking trail on pristine snow.

Liam led them higher up the mountain, and Ellie had to concede that having the snowmobile made the climb much easier.

Despite her reluctance to have Liam with her, she was glad to have him there.

ONCE LIAM FELT that Ellie could handle the snowmobile, he let her take the lead. After forty-five minutes he estimated that she had led them on a circular path crisscrossing Adler, Thatcher, and Hapgood land. When she stopped at last, he pulled beside her.

"I think you may have scared off every wild animal within a ten-mile radius," he said.

She made a face at him as she shut off her machine and removed her helmet. "These are more fun than I thought they'd be." She nodded to the west. "I'm gonna check out that pass."

She took off trudging through ankle deep snow, and he had to scramble to catch up.

"Maybe Eustace isn't of sound mind anymore," she said.

"He seemed alert enough to me."

"Why do you think he wants to see the four of us?"

"He's always been a bit eccentric, but maybe he just wants some company."

"Maybe," she said. "Remember when he appeared in the woods out of nowhere and scared us?"

Liam laughed. "I think I had a heart attack."

"And then you boasted of your boxing skills and how you'd take the old man down if he tried to do us harm."

"I was trying to look out for you."

"And it was appreciated," she said. "What was it like seeing Jennifer again?"

"I'm not sure what you mean," Liam hedged.

"You two dated. And I was friends with her after. I think she was broken up when it ended."

He wasn't sure how to respond since it had been so long ago. He and Jen had been nothing more than a passing fling. Once she had gone home after her ski holiday, it had easily slid away.

"Maybe you should ask her out for coffee," Ellie suggested.

"Maybe she's married."

"True. So you're saying if she's not married or has a boyfriend, then you would ask her out. For coffee." She added the last bit as if for clarity.

"No. And what about Mark? You dated him, so maybe you should get coffee together." As soon as he said it, he hated the image it presented.

She scoffed. "Me and Mark? We were never a thing."

"That's not what he thought." Liam clearly remembered running interference for Ellie at the ball five years ago when Mark had still been pursuing her. "Has he been bothering you again?"

"If you discount his idea of flirting, then no. Not really."

"I'm happy to run interference again, if you need it."

She looked at him like his mother sometimes had when he had been younger. It was a look of *I don't believe you.*

She stopped abruptly when a dilapidated cabin came into view.

"What's this?" she said.

"I don't know."

"Are we on Adler land?"

"To be honest, I have no idea."

She pulled out her camera and started snapping photos. As they approached, a light snowfall blanketed them.

"This place looks old," he said. It appeared hand-hewn and pieced together like Lincoln logs.

"Do you think we can enter?"

He tried the front door, and it gave way. He pushed it back and had to duck to peek inside, the frame was so low. Muted gray light filtered in through the two windows in the front. Luckily no animal greeted them, so he waved for Ellie to follow. She had to bow forward to come inside as well.

"This place is old," she whispered, as if a loud voice might disturb unseen spirits.

He didn't disagree with her assessment. The one-room cabin contained two abandoned wooden bedframes with fraying ropes that had once been the supports, a broken chair and sideboard that looked well-used and handmade, and a thick layer of dust coated the entire place.

They carefully stepped on the floorboards—Liam worried one might give way if they were rotted—and the only sound was the occasional click of Ellie's camera.

"This must've been built in the 1800's," she said.

"Maybe," he murmured. There was something tranquil about the place, as if time stood still here.

Ellie opened a drawer in the sideboard and retrieved something.

"Liam, look at this."

He came to her side, a pile of photos in her hand. The first was a tintype photo of two men. She flipped it over. Someone had written Charlie Thatcher and Henry Adler on the back in block lettering.

"These must be our ancestors," she said.

"Interesting." Leaning close, Liam was suddenly aware of everything Ellie—the scent of her hair and the curve of her cheek and the way she warmed the space around him.

The wanting slammed into him. Shocked, he stepped back, putting space between them.

Ellie pretended not to notice as she inspected the remaining photos one by one, but Liam knew that *she* knew.

The only thing they could do was ignore it. One Adler pursuing a Thatcher was enough, and Ryan clearly had dibs. Besides, Ellie Thatcher—while beautiful and compelling and quite honestly the most interesting female in these parts—would be a complication not worth dealing with.

She handed him the photos when she had finished looking through them, not meeting his eyes.

Several were of the land—forests and the view from this location—along with a photo of the cabin when it was half-built.

But the last photo was the most intriguing. The image was fuzzy, but it was clearly a herd of reindeer. White reindeer.

"Wait," he said. "Is this what I think it is?"

She met his gaze this time. "The herd was real."

"Ellie, this photo could have been taken anywhere else. Probably Finland."

"Maybe," she said, moving close to him again. "But look at this background." She pointed to it then took the photos from his hand, her fingers brushing his, and shuffled back to a different one. "It looks the same as this one, and this view is definitely Reindeer Pass. And look at this." She pointed to one of the animals. "A large female, maybe?"

She smiled at him, and he was aware again of her proximity.

"The Vaadin," he said, his gaze dropping to her mouth of its own free will. He stepped back again before he did something foolish. Like kiss her. "It wouldn't be the same animal today," he added.

"Of course not. Captive reindeer live about twenty years at best. In the wild, the number is much lower. But still, it means the herd was once here. Maybe they kept breeding."

"With each other?" He raised an eyebrow in skepticism. "That wouldn't help their gene pool."

"No, but maybe they interbred with the local deer population. It might've made the offspring stronger."

"True, but perhaps no longer with white fur."

"Yes, but remember what Eustace told us years ago. He said that he'd seen the Vaadin with his wife. And my grandparents also saw it."

"What did they say? Did they confirm it?"

Ellie shrugged. "Grandma was rather vague. She said she wasn't sure what she saw, and that Eustace had a habit of embellishing things. Grandpa Adam said he didn't notice any reindeer because his eyes were only for Grandma." A blush crept onto her cheeks, and she added in a low voice, "I think they were fooling around in the forest, so I didn't press any further. But the feud began shortly thereafter, and then my grandpa gave his share of the reindeer farm to your grandfather."

"Solid reporting, Thatcher."

She gave a grunt of exasperation, her cheeks still rosy and the tip of her nose red. It was freezing inside the cabin. "Why are you so skeptical, Liam?"

"Just trying to keep you from being disappointed."

"But don't you think your family—and mine—might like to know what's back here? And this cabin needs to be preserved."

Liam nodded. "You're right. We should determine whose land this is though. I'll get a survey done."

"So practical."

"Thank you. We should do it anyway. This business with Eustace's property is going to get complicated, no doubt."

"I suppose." She glanced at the photos he held. "Do you think I could keep these?"

"Sure." He handed them back to her.

"I'll have a set made for your family." She tucked them into her backpack, then took down an antler rack collecting dust on a shelf. "*Rangifer tarandus*."

"What's that?" he asked.

"The scientific name of reindeer. I was quite obsessed with them when I was younger."

"I remember."

"Did you know reindeer can see things humans can't?"

"Like spirits?"

She laughed, and he liked it. "Maybe. They're the only mammal that can see ultraviolet light. It's thought that it helps them find food, especially in snow conditions."

"It probably helps them to hide so well." He checked

his watch. "We'd better get back out there if you want to get any photos before we have to be at Eustace's place."

Ellie gave the cabin one final inspection, like a college girl trying to decide how to decorate her dorm room, then walked outside.

Liam followed, but not before he decided that he would be back.

Six

Ellie climbed out of Liam's SUV along the road to Eustace's cabin. Liam hadn't wanted to go clear to the end, worried that he might get stuck with the trailer.

After they'd found the other cabin, they had spent the next few hours walking through the forest, and while she had photographed a few animals—several hares, an eagle, and even a fox—they found not one reindeer, not even a garden-variety mule deer.

Ellie left her backpack in the car but grabbed her camera. She had only been to the Buckley Cabin once before, but it might be worth photographing.

An old truck was parked in front, so it appeared that Eustace was home. As they stepped onto the porch, a dark brown lab came tearing around the corner of the cabin.

Ellie had just enough time to shift the camera strap so her very expensive equipment rested on her back as the animal jumped on her, tail wagging so hard she yo-yo-ed back and forth.

"You must be Lilja," Ellie exclaimed.

The front door swung open. "I see you two have met. I told her you were her new mother. She's not one to dwell on the past."

Ellie was laughing as the dog slobbered her with kisses, and she finally was forced to stand to catch her breath. "You didn't say she was young."

Eustace shrugged. "I don't know how old she is."

"She has a lot of energy, so she's young."

"Is that a problem?"

"No. Well, I don't know. I'm staying with my folks. I'll have to check with them before I can fully commit." Ellie shifted the camera in front of her. "Would it be okay if I took some pictures?"

"Suit yourself. C'mon in. You're the first to arrive."

After loving on Ellie, the animal turned her affection to Liam, and it warmed Ellie's heart to see him turn to putty in the dog's hands, or paws as it were. She covertly snapped some photos of the two.

As they stepped into the mudroom Lilja bounded inside.

"I'll make some tea," Eustace said, much like he had the last time Ellie had been here. He headed to the kitchen.

The place hadn't changed much—the living room looked cozy and well-lived in with a fire going in the hearth and a collection of deer antlers crowding the mantel. The reindeer quilt spread across the sofa was the same as before. Ellie took a few photos and then spent several minutes trying to get a good shot of Lilja.

Liam was looking at Eustace's bookshelf along one wall, finally saying over his shoulder, "She's never gonna calm down until you do."

Ellie indulged in a slight eye roll since Liam's back was to her. She was about to get a good angle of the boisterous dog when a knock on the door drove the girl into another frenzy of activity as she ran into the mudroom at the same time as Liam, almost tripping him. He swore under his breath, giving Ellie smug satisfaction.

It was easier this way, since liking Liam wasn't an option. There had been a solid moment in that other cabin when she'd thought he might kiss her. Or maybe she'd wanted to kiss *him*. It was already becoming unclear. It didn't help that she found everything about Liam to be … interesting. She huffed at this moment of holiday lunacy. Like pursuing him was ever going to be an option. Her grandfather would disown her, and then *his* grandfather would try to run her out of town.

Best to keep this attraction to a low simmer—tolerable, a little fun, and definitely not a threat to her sanity. She'd had a few relationships that ticked that box, and she wasn't doing it again.

The chatter of voices announced the arrival of Mark and Jennifer. Lilja bounced with excitement but finally settled down when Eustace gave her a chew bone, which she enjoyed on a dog bed placed near the fireplace.

He carried a tray with a teapot, cups, and a plate of cookies, which Liam quickly took from him and set on the coffee table. Eustace and Mark each took a chair while Jennifer jumped between Liam and Ellie and sat on the sofa with them. Ellie pretended not to notice the maneuver because surely the woman hadn't done it on purpose. So why was Ellie feeling a stab of jealousy?

Ellie took a sip of her drink, a black tea with a hint of cinnamon, appreciating that it was piping hot after spending most of the day outside in the cold. She also appreciated that it wasn't cider, which he had served the last time she'd been here. She wasn't a fan of apples. She reached for a cookie and a bite released a sound of approval from her.

"These are delicious, Eustace," Ellie said, the white chocolate chips and pecans blending perfectly with something else she couldn't quite put her finger on. "What's the secret ingredient?"

Eustace chuckled. "Maple syrup. A favorite recipe of my wife."

When Ellie finished the first one, she reached for a second. She always ate when she was nervous, and watching Jennifer and Liam from the corner of her eye caused an odd sort of anxiety to fill her.

"I'll have to tell Bella," she said.

"So, what's all this about?" Mark asked.

Eustace stirred a spoonful of sugar into his tea. "I've come to realize that it might be time for me to leave."

"The earthly plane?" Ellie asked, a bit horrified that he would speak so nonchalantly about his own death.

Eustace gave her a perplexed look beneath his bushy eyebrows. "No, no. It's just getting harder to keep the place. But here's the thing. I won't sell it to just anyone. The highest price isn't necessarily a good gauge on who should have this land. Now, I know that all your families are interested in it, so here's what I'm gonna do. I'm gonna let the reindeer decide."

"Pardon me?" Jennifer asked, setting down her plate with her cookie half-eaten.

Ellie eyed it, wondering if the woman was going to finish it, since the main cookie plate was now empty.

"Dora and I never had any children. It was a source of great grief for her, for us both, and I hope in the ever-after that I can make it up to her. But having you kids here would make her happy, I think."

Mark leaned forward. "You're going to sell to all of us?"

The gears were all but whirring in his brain. He was

certain he could convince the rest of them to sell off their shares to him. Ellie knew at that moment she would never do it.

Eustace considered it. "That's a thought but seeing as how the Thatchers and Adlers don't get along, you'd all have a built-in feud in trying to divvy it up. And the one thing I ask is that you don't divide the property. My Dora's final resting place is here. I don't want her disturbed. So that brings me to the Vaadin. Whoever sees her first can have my land."

The room was silent except for Lilja's vigorous gnawing of her bone and the crackle of burning wood from the fireplace.

"But I thought the Vaadin wasn't real," Jennifer said, her voice quiet as if children everywhere might overhear her.

"What made you think that?" Eustace asked.

Jennifer looked at Ellie, her mouth ajar. There had been a time when they'd been friends and Ellie had found her intriguing and a bit worldly—she was from Denver and four years older. But now Ellie found her a bit too flashy, too markety. Or something like that.

"Because it's just a story, Eustace," Jennifer said. "And it's a cute story, one that children love. Gosh knows we're making some good money off it. But this is a little silly, don't you think?"

Ellie sneaked a glance at Liam sitting at the other end of the sofa, remaining quiet. They locked eyes, and he gave her a bemused smile.

"Well then, this might be a challenge for you, Jennifer," Eustace said.

"Wait," Mark cut in. "You're saying you'll give your land for free to whoever sees the Vaadin?"

"For free?" Eustace chuckled. "I haven't lost my mind,

son. Of course it's not for free. I need to fund my future, you know."

Ellie had to address the most obvious problem with this scenario. "But you said the Vaadin only appears to couples who are in love. That it's a sign of true love. That means none of us would be able to see it."

"Why would you say that?" Eustace countered.

Another marked silence descended. Clearly everyone was contemplating this question.

"Because none of us are in love with each other." The words squeaked out of Ellie against her will. Why must she state the obvious?

"Well, I don't profess to know how this might all work," Eustace said. "But the myth of the Vaadin is strong in this area, and all myths are based in truth. And this land, this very area, was the original Reindeer Pass of the town, so I cannot in good conscience sell to someone who won't honor it." He held up a hand. "And I know you all will profess to do so, but sometimes our words don't match our heart. I need to be sure. So humor an old man."

"What exactly are you saying?" Jennifer sputtered. "That I'm supposed to go into the mountains looking for a giant reindeer that most assuredly doesn't exist anymore? It's the middle of winter. We could all die out there."

Ellie hadn't realized how much of a whiner Jennifer was.

Eustace chuckled and set his tea on the side table and settled into the stuffed chair. He threaded his fingers and rested them on his belly. "You've all grown up here. I wouldn't send you out there if I didn't think you had the skills to do it."

Jennifer shook her head, clearly frustrated by the turn of the conversation.

"There is magic in this world," Eustace continued.

"Why do you think I didn't stop you from using the Vaadin to market your park?"

She shrugged.

"The Vaadin isn't meant to belong to one person over another. It's for all. Like Santa Claus. You would never claim Santa as your own, would you?"

"How will you know if someone is telling the truth about seeing her?" Ellie asked, thinking specifically of Mark. She offered a glare in his direction to let him know she was onto him, but he didn't notice.

"How about a picture?" Eustace said. "And I give permission for you all to be on my land."

"So it *is* on your land," Jennifer said pointedly.

Eustace shrugged. "It's a big mountain."

"Didn't you say you saw it with your wife?" Mark pressed. "Where was that?"

"Not far from here." Eustace waved a hand.

"All right then." Mark stood. "I guess we're done here. I need to get back to the village."

Ellie wondered if Mark wanted another private powwow with the four of them to figure out a way around this strange instruction from Eustace, but he took off.

Jennifer lingered, talking to Liam outside while Ellie stood at the doorway, saying goodbye to Eustace and Lilja. "I'll talk to my mom about the dog," she said, falling more in love with the mutt every second.

Eustace smiled. "I think she likes you."

"Thank you for the tea and cookies."

Eustace crossed his arms, glancing at Liam and Jennifer in the distance. Ellie didn't turn around, not really wanting to watch them flirt with each other, if that was in fact happening.

"Ellie Thatcher, the girl who loved the reindeer."

"What makes you say that?"

"I heard the stories about you. How you searched for the Arctic herd when you were a girl."

"Have you seen them?" she asked. When he paused, her pulse kicked up. "They do exist, don't they?"

"Truthfully, I'm not sure. I've only seen regular reindeer in these parts."

"Is there anything regular about reindeer?"

He smiled. "No, I reckon not."

"If you haven't seen the white herd, then why the search for the Vaadin?"

"Because there's more to this life than what you see with your eyes."

Her shoulders sagged a bit. He *was* sending them on a wild goose chase, wasn't he. And while she wanted to believe in something bigger and grander in the world; in truth he was an old man who might've spent too much time alone in the mountains after the death of his wife.

"Eustace, you should get out more," she suggested. "The Reindeer Ball is next weekend. You should attend."

"With you?" he teased. "Are you asking me on a date, young lady?"

She laughed. "I'm not going, but I'm sure the Osborns would be happy to accompany you." She knew that Mark's parents had long looked after Eustace. Despite Mark's ambitions for land and wealth, his family was good people.

Eustace nodded. "I'll think about it." He looked past her shoulder again. "Stewardship of the land is very important. I learned that all those years ago when I worked with both the Thatchers and the Adlers, before your two families decided bitterness was a better condition than friendship."

He wasn't wrong, but the feud between her grandfather and Liam's grandfather was beyond her control. And for the longest time, she hadn't really cared too much about it.

It had little effect except that she and her brothers had been told to stay away from the Adler boys, but they hadn't done that.

Maybe it was time she did care.

"I'll give you a hint about the Vaadin," Eustace said. "To find her, you'll need to believe."

"In what?" Ellie asked.

"In magic. In yourself. And in true love."

Ellie shifted uncomfortably, and she glanced over her shoulder at Liam. He was laughing at something Jennifer had said, their demeanor relaxed. They appeared comfortable with each other, and she wondered why *that* Liam was never present when Ellie was with him.

When Eustace had first told her and Liam about the Vaadin, she'd been sixteen and Liam an aloof twenty-one-year-old, and she'd had to ignore the spark she'd felt sitting beside him on Eustace's sofa. She'd sat on the same sofa minutes ago and hadn't felt a thing, except irritation that Jennifer was sandwiched between them.

She really needed to get her head out of the clouds. Perhaps it was a side effect of coming home, that she reverted to that young girl she'd been, filled with romantic and fanciful notions, like magical reindeer and the aggravating Adler boys. The aggravating Liam Adler.

She cleared her throat. "Eustace, can I just clarify that anyone can see the Vaadin, right? You don't have to be part of a couple?"

He shrugged. "I guess we'll find out."

Ellie said farewell, along with a goodbye ear scratch to Lilja, and reluctantly approached Liam and Jennifer's private conversation. Jennifer responded by suggesting that she and Ellie have lunch sometime.

Then Ellie was back in Liam's SUV, the snowmobiles

loaded on the trailer, as he drove her back down the mountain.

"You and Jennifer seem to be hitting it off," she said, adjusting the heating vent so it wasn't blowing directly on her. Perspiration was breaking out on the nape of her neck.

Liam glanced at her. "I suppose."

"You better watch out. All those old feelings will come back." Another thought occurred to her. "And then you'll both see the Vaadin."

"What?"

"Only those experiencing true love see the reindeer."

Liam laughed. "You think Jennifer is my true love?"

Ellie made a noncommittal sound and looked out the window.

"And then what happens?" he asked. "Do she and I share the property? I doubt Gramps wants to be related to the Dixons."

"Why? Is he feuding with them as well?"

"You've met my grandfather, right? Making friends is not his strong suit."

"I guess I can see that," Ellie said. "But if you're married, he'd have to make an exception."

"Married? You think I'm gonna marry Jennifer Dixon?"

"Are you?" However, she wasn't sure she wanted to know the answer.

"No." He glanced at her again. "What happens if you and Mark see the Vaadin? Are you gonna marry him?"

She snorted. "No."

"I mean, you dated him about as long as I dated Jennifer."

"I didn't *date* him. We went out twice and nothing happened. I'm sure you can't say the same about her."

Liam gave her the oddest look, and she immediately regretted the turn of the conversation.

"Wait a minute. Are you jealous, Thatcher?"

She huffed. "No."

"What would happen if you and I both see this mythical Vaadin?" he asked. "Will I have to marry you?"

"Our grandfathers' heads would explode. I, for one, will not be responsible for that." Not exactly a refusal. With hope, Liam didn't notice. "If that happens, we'll toss a coin to see who gets the land."

"You think the grandfathers would go for that?"

Ellie sighed. "The grandfathers are gonna think Eustace is bananas."

"I think Eustace would refute that by saying the grandfathers are crazy."

"No, what he actually said was they let bitterness replace friendship."

"And you wonder why I never wanted to return home," Liam said. "It's easier not being in the middle of this."

Ellie couldn't dispute that, but as they drove into Barstow, her mood brightened considerably.

This place, and Reindeer Pass, were home.

Seven

"How long has it been?" Jennifer asked.

Ellie sat with her at a table in Bella's Bakery. It was Monday and the lunch crowd was bustling. Bella's mom—Ellie's Aunt Sara—was behind the counter helping Bella. Ellie warmed her hands on her mug, sipping her latte as a heavy snowfall blanketed the street outside.

Her Grand Opening of the studio was today and this morning she'd had exactly zero customers, so when Jennifer had called, she'd figured she could indulge in a long lunch.

"Five years, I think," Ellie said.

"It's wild that we're all back in town." No doubt the *we* was including Liam.

Bella delivered their lunch—a roast beef sandwich for Ellie and a bowl of homemade vegetable soup for Jennifer. "Anything else, guys?" Bella asked.

"No," Ellie said as Jennifer shook her head. "Thanks, Bells."

As they dug into their food, Ellie asked, "I'm surprised

you decided to move here full-time. It must be a big change from Denver."

"That's for sure." Jennifer tucked her hair behind an ear. She'd left it down today and Ellie envied the ease with which the woman carried herself. She had to concede she could see why Liam had liked her back then and might still like her today, their conversation in the car Saturday afternoon notwithstanding.

Ellie hadn't seen him yesterday. She'd been unable to get into the mountains because her mom had wanted to go Christmas shopping for last-minute items, and as Ellie had completed no holiday purchases, she'd agreed to spend the day together in Durango. By early afternoon, snow had begun to fall and had been steady ever since, silently crushing Ellie's hope of getting back out there.

"I went through a terrible divorce," Jennifer continued between bites of soup. "And he kind of cleaned me out."

"I'm so sorry."

"Well, I needed a place to land, and my parents have a condo here they purchased three years ago. They let me move in, and now that my dad's retired, we're all cohabiting. I'd like to move, of course. Eustace's land would help."

"But it's so remote. Would you really like living there?"

"Oh, I'm not gonna do that. I'd flip it. I have a contact at the ski resort, and I think I can get a good deal."

Ellie took a break from her meal since Jennifer's admission was leaving her stomach a bit sour.

Jennifer took a sip of her ice water. "So what's the deal with Liam?"

The sour knot in Ellie's belly was swiftly ruining her appetite. "What do you mean?"

"Why were you both *really* together on Saturday?"

Ellie shouldn't have been surprised by Jennifer's interest

in Liam. It had been perfectly obvious the other day. But disappointment filled her. Not because she was jealous, as Liam had accused, but because it made Ellie feel a bit used.

She plastered a bright smile on her face. "Just the usual from Grandpa Adler. He was afraid I'd trespass on Adler land while taking pictures. He sent Liam to babysit me."

"Sounds typical. Liam looks good, doesn't he?"

Yes. But instead, Ellie replied, "I suppose."

"Is he married?"

"No."

"Girlfriend?"

"I don't think so." Ellie tried to keep her expression neutral, because Jennifer's questioning was making her fidget. "Why? Are you thinking of going after him again?"

"Maybe?" Jennifer's expression was less enthusiastic and more calculating. "After my divorce I decided no more deadbeats."

"You want Liam for his money?"

Jennifer seemed exasperated. "I'm not that shallow. But Liam's a catch, and I have to look out for my future. No one else will. Would you help me?"

A sense of foreboding settled over Ellie. "With what?"

"Maybe put in a good word for me."

"You seem to think Liam and I are friends. We're enemies, remember?"

"The feud." Jennifer nodded. "Of course. But he's always had a soft spot for you. After you saved me from the tree well, he was, oh I don't know, he was protective of you."

Oh.

"Will you go into the mountains again with him?" she continued.

"Maybe." Ellie had no idea.

Jennifer's mouth pinched in frustration. "I'll be honest, Ellie. I don't want to go into the woods looking for some reindeer ghost, so maybe I could go with you and Liam?"

Ellie could think of no reason to say no, except that if they were all together then who would get credit for seeing the Vaadin?

Did she really think the Vaadin was real? Her heart whispered yes.

"Sure," Ellie said, taking a sip of her latte. "We should invite Mark too." He could be a distraction so Ellie wouldn't have to watch Jennifer and Liam rekindle their long dormant romance.

"We all know the Vaadin isn't real," Jennifer said. "It's more of a spirit thing, like Santa Claus. You looked for it for years and never found it, right?"

"Right. And you're probably correct about the true nature of the Vaadin." Ellie didn't feel like mentioning that one time with Liam when she thought she'd seen something.

Having just picked up a coffee to go, Mark approached their table.

"Are we teaming up?" he asked, taking a seat. "If so, then I want in. Because we need to figure out a way around this obstacle that Eustace has put in our path."

"What if it's valid?" Ellie asked, mostly to irritate him.

"Do you think there's actually Arctic reindeer back in the mountains?" he asked. "Eustace is eccentric, but I never thought he'd be this off his rocker."

"You're just mad that he didn't pick you right off the bat," Jennifer said.

"My parents have been good friends with him for a long time. That ought to count for something."

Jennifer pushed her empty soup bowl to the center of the table. "Maybe we have nothing to worry about with

Eustace's plan. No one will see the Vaadin, and ultimately, he'll have to sell the old-fashioned way—to the buyer with the best offer. Maybe we should all agree *not* to search."

"True," Mark said. "It will all shake down in the end."

"Shake down to what?" Ellie asked.

"He'll pass away, and the land will likely go to my parents. He doesn't have any children, and he's always been close with my folks."

Wouldn't they have to be in Eustace's will? Did the old man even have a will?

Liam pushed open the door to the bakery and brushed snow off his shoulders and hair. His eyes locked on Ellie's.

"Why do I feel like I'm missing an important meeting?" he said.

"It's nice to see you again, Liam," Jennifer beamed. "Why don't you join us?"

Ellie grabbed her latte, which had thankfully cooled to lukewarm, and had a long drink.

He removed his wool coat and scarf, draping them on a chair, and sat with his leg bumping Ellie's, causing a hotspot to form on her knee. She shifted so it wouldn't seem as if she were enjoying it because she wasn't.

She crossed her legs and said, "I'm sure it's no surprise, but we were just discussing Eustace's property."

He scanned the table, his expression amused. "Trying to come up with a way to game the system?"

"If you've got one," Jennifer answered, "then I'm all ears."

"I think you're all missing the point." Liam leaned back in his chair. "We're all competitors. Helping each other is off the table."

Jennifer laughed. "So cynical, Liam. Some things never change. Let's change the subject. Who's going to the Reindeer Ball? Liam?"

"Yep, for my mom."

"I'm sure it will be hard for her this year having lost your dad. Please let her know that if she needs any help, I'm happy to contribute. Ellie, I almost forgot. My brother, David, is coming the day after tomorrow, and I think you two would hit it off. You're not seeing anyone, are you? Maybe you could go to the ball together?"

In the years the Dixon family had come to the area for ski trips, Ellie had never met David, but it didn't matter. She wasn't looking for a date.

"That's nice of you, but—"

"Ellie's going with me," Liam interrupted.

Although his voice was calm, there was a flash of heat in Liam's gaze that momentarily stunned her.

"She is?" Jennifer asked, and Ellie didn't miss the hurt expression on her face considering the conversation they'd just had.

Ellie wanted to set the record straight, but she also had no desire to go on a blind date with Jennifer's brother. "Well—"

Liam cut her off. "My mother wants her to photograph the decorations, and I have to help with set up, so it worked out for me to take her." He slid a look to Ellie that was … hopeful.

Once again, Liam was coming to her rescue when it came to the Reindeer Ball, pretending to be her date. It *was* pretend, wasn't it?

"Oh, that makes sense." Jennifer's face relaxed. "But everyone is going to think we've entered a time warp with Adlers and Thatchers acting as if they like each other."

Feeling a bit guilty about the lie, Ellie sought to change the subject. "I think Eustace is interested in going." She looked at Mark. "Would your parents help with the logistics?"

"I can ask them," Mark said.

"I'll take care of Eustace," Jennifer offered. "He can be *my* date."

Mark sighed. "You're just trying to get on his good side."

"Every little bit helps. But Ellie's right. He deserves a night out." She cleared her throat. "Liam, maybe you could come by my folks' place for dinner this week. They'd love to see you."

Liam's normally stoic façade faltered. "Sure, I'll check my schedule."

"I didn't realize there were so many dates to be made at this time of year," Mark said, looking at Ellie. "How about dinner? For old times' sake?"

What was happening?

"My schedule is full."

"With what?" he asked.

"Aside from a dozen Christmas commitments with my family, I'm planning to spend every spare minute in the mountains."

Or maybe she'd head there now and stay until after New Year's.

Eight

The following morning, Liam got an early start at the new office in Barstow, helping the movers carry and organize boxes and office equipment. By the time everything had been shifted to the large second story, Ellie's photography studio was lit up with the OPEN sign facing outward. Liam entered, the bell on the door ringing.

She stood up from behind the counter, wearing an oversized cream sweater with a high turtleneck, her hair flowing in soft curls. She seemed a bit taken aback to see him.

"Did you go on a run?" she asked.

He glanced down at his sweatpants, sneakers, and pullover. "No. We moved in upstairs this morning."

"Need any help?"

"Thanks for the offer, but no. We hired a couple guys to move the big stuff. We still have some boxes of files and a lot of organizing to do, but Mrs. Scott has worked for Gramps for years and she'll do most of that."

"Then I guess you're free to go on that run," she teased.

"About yesterday. I didn't mean to corner you into going to the ball with me."

Liam had needed to leave for a meeting after the impromptu lunch date with Ellie, Jennifer, and Mark and didn't have a chance to talk to her. He'd thought about texting her last night but then decided to speak to her in person today.

"No, it's okay," she said. "I'm sure Jennifer's brother is very nice, but I'm not looking to be set up."

"I kind of figured. Look, I talked to my mom about you photographing the ball, and she's definitely up for it. So if you're interested ...."

"Yes! Absolutely."

"Great." He pulled out his phone. "I'll text you her email and you can let her know your rates."

Her phone dinged when she received the message.

"I also have something for you." He set the book he'd been holding on the counter.

"What's this?" she asked.

"I had a survey done yesterday on the property lines around Eustace's house as well as the old cabin we found."

"And?"

"The cabin sits on Hapgood land."

She frowned. "Huh. But clearly it was inhabited by a Thatcher and probably an Adler too."

"I agree, and I think this book proves it. I found it inside the cupboard."

She opened the cover. "You went back?"

"I guess I'm a curious soul."

"Careful, Liam. You might be turning into a romantic."

She wasn't looking at him, so he indulged watching her. "Maybe."

She gasped. "This is a journal by my great-great grandmother."

"I figured." The name in the front—Eleonoora Korhonen Thatcher—was a dead giveaway. "But it's not written in English."

Ellie carefully turned the pages. "It's Finnish."

"How do you know?"

"When I lived in Finland, I started studying the language."

"Maybe you can translate it."

"Maybe," she said quietly. "My skill level is fairly basic." She raised her gaze. "If there's clues about the Vaadin in here, I could have the upper hand."

"I guess I'll take that risk."

The bell rang as the door opened and a mother with three young children entered, looking a bit frazzled.

"I'll be right with you," Ellie said to the woman.

Liam reluctantly took that as his cue to leave. "See you around, Thatcher."

"Bye, Liam."

Ellie was feeling warm and happy throughout the photoshoot with the three kids, despite their rambunctiousness and general lack of focus in getting a photo done in their Christmas best. It was about the journal Ellie kept saying to herself, but in truth it was about Liam.

He continually was being nice to her, and it was messing with her determination to keep him at arm's length.

Once the harried-looking mother and her children had left—they'd been begging for a hot chocolate at Bella's—Ellie's mom waved from the street and came inside, wearing a trendy knit poncho and tiny Christmas ornaments dangling from her ears. Her brown hair was tucked into a lush tan-colored hat with a wide brim of alpaca fur, making her look like a Mongolian herdsman, but Ellie didn't point that out. Her mom loved that hat.

"Hi, sweetie! How's business?"

"It's coming along. I finally have a few bookings."

"That's wonderful." While Ellie and her brothers often teased their mom about her eternal optimism, it was a blessing every day to see her smiling face.

"Listen, Mom, I'm glad you stopped by. I was going to talk with you this morning, but you'd already left."

"Grandma Izzie wanted to get an early start in distributing the holiday donations. What's up?"

Ellie debated what to start with but decided not to lead with Lilja.

"Mrs. Adler would like me to shoot the Reindeer Ball, and I'm thinking of saying yes. Would that be okay with Grandma and Grandpa?"

"You could ask them, but yes, why not? I've been trying to convince your father to go. I don't think it has anything to do with the Adlers but more the fact that he doesn't like getting dressed up. But if his little girl will be there, that'll change his mind."

"Haven't you gone to every ball since it began?"

"Well, we went to two. You were there for the first one when there was that fiasco between you and Liam Adler. He's a nice boy."

"I don't think he's a boy anymore, Mom. I forgot to mention that he and Ryan now own this building, so I'm leasing from Adler Inc."

"Well, aren't you keeping secrets." But her mom smirked with amusement. "Does Grandpa know?"

"Yes."

"Hmm. Maybe there's hope to end this feud after all. Well, we should go to the ball then. I'll get some tickets. And you need to get a dress."

Ugh. Right. A dress.

"I'll talk to Bella," Ellie said. "Maybe she has one I can borrow."

"If not, there's a new boutique called Marie's near the ski resort. She might have something."

Ellie nodded. "Okay, the second thing is … can I get a dog?"

"A dog? You just got back. Don't you think you should get settled first?"

"Eustace Hapgood has the cutest chocolate lab that just showed up one day, and he can't find the owner, if there ever was one, and he says he can't keep her."

Her mother sighed. "You know that Nanna is coming the day after tomorrow, right?"

Nanna. Right. Ellie had forgotten, and she knew where her mother was going with this.

"My mother is terribly allergic to dogs," she said. "I can't bring one into the house while she stays with us."

"No, you're right. How long is she visiting?"

"She's leaving the day after New Year's."

That was more than two weeks from now.

"Okay. I'll figure something out." Maybe Eustace could keep Lilja until then.

"Was there anything else?" her mom asked.

Ellie pushed the journal across the counter. "This."

Her mom carefully opened the book. When she saw the owner's name written inside the front cover, she said, "Where on earth did you get this?"

"It's a long story."

"Eleonoora Thatcher," her mom murmured. "You know you're named after her, right?"

Ellie nodded, saying a bit sarcastically, "Yes, I know." She'd heard this throughout her childhood.

"All right, cheeky girl. No reason to have an attitude."

"Sorry."

"You're just sore about the dog. I'll talk to your father and see if there's something we can do."

"Thanks, Mom."

"I think this is all in Finnish."

"I can probably translate some of it," Ellie said, "but would you know anyone else who can speak it?"

"Grandpa Adam."

"He speaks Finnish?"

"He does."

"Why didn't I know this?" Ellie asked.

"Well, he hasn't in a long time, so he may be a bit rusty. In fact, I believe it was Eleonoora who taught him."

"He knew her?"

Her mother nodded. "She died when he was a teenager. He's spoken of it before. Weren't you listening?"

"I guess not. Maybe I couldn't hear anything past Owen and Jamie always dominating the airwaves."

"Speaking of which. Your brothers are coming in a day early, so we're going to the grandparents for dinner." She tapped the book. "You should bring this. Now I need to go. I'm off to Bella's to get some cookies for my bunco group." Her mom leaned over the counter and gave her a hug, then left.

Ellie started reading the journal, making notes on a pad. She could at least try to translate as much as possible before talking to her grandfather.

Her cellphone rang, the ringtone playing Mariah Carey's "All I Want For Christmas Is You." It was Liam.

"Hi," she said.

"Can you meet me at the reindeer farm at three o'clock?" he said without preamble.

"Why?"

"We're getting a delivery, and I think you might be interested."

"What is it?"

"I'd rather not say, in case it falls through," he replied. "But I think you're going to want to be there."

"Shall I wear a disguise?" she asked.

"Did you when you were an employee?"

"Of course not."

"There's your answer. See you then, Ellie."

He hadn't called her "Thatcher" this time. Hearing her given name on his lips did something funny to her insides, like when as a child she would step outside the house knowing her brothers were lying in wait to pummel her with snowballs, but she'd go anyway. She had never been one to cower and let life pass her by.

If she was leaving at three, more like two-thirty since she would need time to drive to the farm, then she would have to work on the journal later. She had the photoshoot from earlier to edit. With Christmas so close, the few customers she had wanted their photos ASAP.

Nine

Ellie pulled up to the Adler Reindeer Farm, having traversed the cinder-covered road to Reindeer Pass. Today was overcast so it seemed likely there'd be snow in the immediate forecast. While she looked forward to seeing her brothers later, she also wanted to curl up with Eleonoora's journal and a cup of hot chocolate. Her parents had a large stone fireplace in the great room, and a roaring fire would be the perfect bookend to the night.

The farm hadn't changed much in the eight years since she'd worked here. The visitor's center was in the same place although the exterior had undergone an overhaul with new siding and a bigger gate at the entrance. Extra outdoor tables had been added for guests to enjoy a hot beverage and a snack while waiting for their tour to begin. Ellie had eventually been promoted to tour guide and she'd remained in that coveted position until she'd had to quit for school in New York City.

She didn't see any sign of Liam, so she went into the visitor center. A young girl was working at the checkout counter, but Ellie didn't know her, so she browsed the adjacent gift shop. The Adlers had embraced the legend of the Vaadin with t-shirts, mugs, and baby bibs covered with a likeness of the magical creature. That Liam hadn't known anything about the Vaadin's commercial success in the area spoke to the fact that he must never come in here.

From behind came a surprised bellow. "Ellie Thatcher?"

She spun around and smiled big. "Mick!"

The manager of the Adler Ranch and Reindeer Farm folded her into a big bear hug, his barn jacket smelling like musky reindeer. Thankfully it was December and not early fall when the bulls would urinate on their hind legs to create a unique and supposedly attractive scent for the females.

"It's good to see you," she said as he released her. The wrinkles on his face were a bit deeper and his beard had lost all color, but his eyes still sparkled with the same energy she remembered.

"You were my best tour guide, you know that, right?"

"And you were the best manager I've ever had. I can't believe you're still here."

"You mean you can't believe I'm still alive," he teased.

"No, of course not," she said sincerely. "But it's a lot of work running this place."

"Don't I know it, but I'd be here even if the Adlers fired me."

"They would never do that." The Adlers valued his skills, and Mick had taught Ellie everything she knew about the animals, igniting a love she'd already had but that his tutelage expanded.

"How was that fancy art school you went to?"

"It was good. I've traveled the world"—she gestured as if she were someone famous—"but now I'm back."

"I always knew you were destined for great things."

She smiled. "Thanks. But I'm back for good now."

"Now why on earth would you do that?"

"You can never truly escape the pull of home."

"There's some truth to that," he said. "My only question is—why did it take you so long?"

Embarrassment filled her that she hadn't come by sooner. It had been tricky when she'd worked here because of the feud, and during subsequent visits home she hadn't been sure if she would be welcome, so she tactfully had stayed away. But maybe that had been a mistake.

"I'm young," she answered. "Give me a bit of grace."

"Amen to that. Would you like to see the reindeer? We've had quite a few births. And I'm sorry to say we lost Sven."

That squeezed her heart. The bull had always been a flirt with females both reindeer and human.

"I'm sorry to hear that," she said. "I saw Ruby up at the Christmas Village."

"She always likes a change of scenery, so we rent her out every season."

"I think she remembered me. She was as loving as ever. But I'm here because Liam Adler asked me to come."

Mick's expression changed to a look of surprise.

"You know why, don't you?" she prodded. "Will you tell me?"

"I'm not sure what to tell you, to be honest. But c'mon. I'll take you to him."

Mick pulled on a red plaid fur trapper hat. She followed him outside and around the corrals to an unloading area off limits to the public. Liam, wearing a dark blue hoodie and jeans, stood with Ryan and his mother. When he saw her, he waved her forward.

Once everyone had exchanged greetings, Ellie asked, "What's going on?"

Liam pulled a paper from his jean pocket and handed it to her. "I was going through some of my dad's things, and I found this inside one of his winter coats."

It was an email from a man named Fredrik Nilsen confirming the purchase of a female Arctic reindeer.

"Is this for real?" she asked, a bit breathless.

"We're not sure," Ryan said, "but the delivery date is today."

Liam's mom added, "I finally checked Teddy's email yesterday and saw a message from Mr. Nilsen. That's when we put it all together."

"You didn't know?" Ellie asked her.

"No. But Teddy liked to surprise us." Her voice broke and her eyes teared up.

Liam put an arm around her. "He's still surprising us."

Ellie glanced at the paper again. "I thought Arctic reindeer were extinct."

"Somehow Dad found one," Ryan said. "He must've reached out to a breeder."

A large truck rumbled down the side road toward them, the vehicle like the kind that transported cattle but smaller. As it neared, the narrow slats impeded a view of the cargo it carried, but Ellie craned her neck to see inside anyway.

The driver pulled to a stop and exited the vehicle. Liam met him and they discussed whatever particulars were important as Ellie moved to the side of the vehicle, catching a sliver of white fur, while the clap of hooves on the truck floor startled her.

The female was large.

Liam signed the delivery agreement, and the driver pulled out the ramp at the back of the truck and secured it.

Ellie crowded alongside Mary Adler and Ryan as Liam and Mick helped unlatch the back gate, swinging it open.

Covered in snowy white fur, the animal was like every child's dream of what Santa's reindeer might have looked like. She was so much taller than any reindeer Ellie had ever seen, the antlers reaching so high they brushed the ceiling of the truck.

"Rudolph *is* real," Ryan said, as everyone stared.

Mary Adler stepped closer. "We all might have to agree that Rudolph was a girl."

A lead ran from a halter to a hook alongside the wall of the truck, so the animal couldn't move but she watched with a spark of intelligence and curiosity in her gaze.

Mesmerized, Ellie couldn't look away. "I can't believe she's come all the way from Finland."

"Dad never did anything halfway," Liam said, as he climbed into the truck with an easy grace.

He carefully approached the reindeer and unhooked the lead, leading the girl down the ramp. Liam was tall but her presence dwarfed him. They all took several steps back to give her some space. Despite her calm demeanor, she was still a wild animal and could react unpredictably. Once Liam had her on the ground, he paused.

"I think we may have found our Vaadin," Liam said.

Ellie craned her neck to look up at the magnificent animal. "Eustace will be so surprised when we tell him."

It had been quite the event at the reindeer farm with the arrival of the magnificent female. Liam was still stunned that she had made it without any issue, having had a long trek to get here, coming all the way from a breeding farm in Lapland, Finland.

While Mick and Ryan had helped get the animal settled in the barn—Ellie and his mother acting the avid spectators—Liam had handled the paperwork, although his father had pretty much taken care of everything regarding payment and import documentation. By the time Liam got to the barn, only Ellie was sitting on a bench across from the new girl's stall, camera in hand as she snapped photos of the newly minted star of the Adler Reindeer Farm.

"Where is everyone?" he asked.

In a quiet voice, Ellie replied, "Your mom had a meeting for the ball, Ryan said he had a date, and Mick had other chores to get to. I hope you don't mind that I stayed."

The reindeer was munching on grain from a trough, periodically lifting her head to look at them before continuing with her meal.

Liam took a seat beside Ellie. The journal he'd given her earlier was atop her bag.

"Have you been able to decipher it?" he asked.

"My day has proved busier than I'd planned, so I've just started. The beginning seems to be about Eleonoora's journey from Finland in 1881 when she accompanied her father and a herd of reindeer en route to America. There were thirteen animals altogether, although one died along the way. They left the Port of Helsinki and sailed to New York. From there they took a train to St. Louis, and then they had to herd the animals to Colorado."

"It must've taken them weeks to get here."

"Three months and seven days."

Liam kept his gaze on the massive reindeer, but he was hyper-aware of Ellie beside him. It felt right to have her here, that somehow her presence had been required today. Perhaps it was why the animal seemed so calm, so accepting of her new environment. As if it were meant to bc.

"No mention of what type of reindeer they were?" he asked.

"Not specifically although she does mention a white-furred breed, but the context is unclear. Today we know them as the East Greenland caribou, and according to some online research, they did go extinct in 1900. So maybe she helped to keep the breed alive in her own way. She refers to something called a *noita* in reference to herself, which can translate to a witch, but I think it more closely aligns with a shaman."

"You sound like you don't believe it."

"She was seventeen. What culture would have a female shaman that was so young?"

Liam chuckled. "Ellie Thatcher, don't be so prejudiced."

"I'm not prejudiced, I'm just skeptical. She also called herself a *runoilija*, which means a poet but back then it was more closely translated to a rune singer. I think such shamans would recite stories orally to heal and to educate. She seemed to have a spiritual connection to the reindeer they brought with them. There was a large female in the herd and Eleonoora called her Lumi, which means 'snow', so maybe she was actually thc color of snow."

"Then maybe we should name our girl Lumi in honor of the one who came before her."

Ellie met his gaze, her usually guarded disposition open and soft. Had Ryan really said he had a date? Had his brother finally convinced Bella to go out with him? And why did Liam feel a stab of envy over it?

He faced forward again, focusing on the reindeer now gracing their presence. The bigger question, of course, was how much longer could he hide his attraction to Ellie?

"Lumi," she said, as if testing it out. "That's nice. Why do you think your father brought her here?"

"I don't know. Maybe he wanted to breed her." Then he reached for a more far-fetched reason. "Or maybe he wanted to heal the rift between our grandfathers."

"That's a thought, except that neither of them are here, so they know nothing of her."

"Shall we invite them both to an unveiling tomorrow?" he asked.

"That would be something." Then she sighed, her humor fading. "I'm not sure I can get Grandpa over here. He's never admitted it in so many words, but he's never expressed much interest in the reindeer. When he gave them all to your grandfather, he was just done with them."

"I suppose we don't need to get involved," Liam said.

"Except that we keep finding ourselves involved."

Her shoulder brushed against him, but he didn't move away. He thought of Ryan and Bella.

"Maybe it's the universe's way of telling us that a Thatcher and an Adler can be friends," he said. *Or more than friends.* It didn't escape Liam that he was a hypocrite after giving Ryan so much grief for pursuing Bella.

"Did Ryan happen to say who his date was with?" he added.

"No. Why?"

"I think it might be your cousin, Bella."

"What?" Her surprised response caused Lumi to startle, a shiver rippling across her snowy hide. "Oh, sorry, girl," Ellie added with a whisper. Then she said more quietly, "Bella never said anything. Are you sure?"

"I'm sure about the way he feels. I can't speak for Bella."

"She would never date an Adler. She honors the feud like a dutiful Thatcher."

"Then you underestimate the charm of the men in our family. Are you a dutiful Thatcher too, Ellie?"

She laughed, refusing to meet his gaze, her movements stiff as she set her camera down and pinched her coat together. Then she blew a stray hair away from her face, the dark strand refusing to cooperate. He was about to reach out and tame it when she suddenly checked her watch.

"Oh no. I'm late." She grabbed the journal and her camera and put each into her canvas bag. "My brothers are in town, and I'm supposed to be at my grandparents' house for dinner."

She gave one last look at Lumi.

"You can come by anytime and see her," he said as they left the barn. Darkness had descended but colorful Christmas lights surrounding the parking lot illuminated their way.

"Thanks. I'd like that. I took a photo to show Eustace, but who saw her first?"

"I'd say it was about even."

"So we'll share his land?"

They stopped at Ellie's car, alone and covered in a thin layer of snow. The farm had closed nearly an hour ago.

"Would that be so bad?" he asked.

"I'm not sure what to do with this nice version of you. Where's Liam the Grinch?"

Did she really believe he was that cold-hearted? He didn't have the luxury of being overly emotional. There was too much to do since the death of his father, along with making sure his mother knew she could count on him. "Grinch, huh?"

"I suppose you're more Grinch-lite." Her cheeks were rosy from more than the cold, and it gave him hope. Ellie

Thatcher felt something for him. She beeped her car to unlock the door, which Liam opened for her.

"Goodnight, Liam."

"Goodnight, Ellie."

He watched her drive away, then returned to the barn and to Lumi, a gift from his father from the grave. He was hit with both renewed grief but also warmth, almost like a hug. His father had never been a particularly demonstrative man—a result no doubt of his grandfather's prickly attitude—but he'd been a good and attentive dad. And the barn seemed filled with … spirit … as if Teddy Adler were here, right now, with Liam.

He blinked back tears as his throat tightened.

"Thanks, Dad."

Maybe the arrival of Lumi had nothing to do with Eustace's property and the myth of the Vaadin, or the Adler Reindeer Farm, or the Thatcher-Adler feud. Maybe it was meant to bring Liam to Ellie.

He'd never believed in magic. It had always been for children, like a younger Ellie when she'd been obsessed with the long-disappeared Arctic reindeer in the surrounding mountains. Her devotion had been amusing to him, and he'd been fond of her back then.

And now, like a quiet snowfall, the fondness had blossomed into something more, and it had taken this damned reindeer to make him see it.

As Lumi watched him, his logical mind told him the reindeer wasn't really involved, that he was simply projecting his own thoughts and wishes onto her, but it were as if he could feel his father and the entire Adler line crowding around him. For the first time since being back his heart swelled with pride about the ancient connection to this place. To his home. And somehow to Ellie.

Did she feel it too?

There was only one way to find out, and he would have to convince her to go against her family's wishes, as well as his own. Ryan and Bella had already jumped headlong in, but would Ellie take the leap? She'd always had an abundance of courage.

Instead of the usual grief about his dad, and the frustration over his life being taken over by Adler Inc., a well of hope spread in Liam's chest.

Ten

Ellie let herself into her grandparents' house since no one heard her knock and followed the din of conversation to the kitchen. Compared to the Adler mansion, Adam and Isabelle lived more modestly, but then the entire family didn't reside together. Their house wasn't far from the Adler Reindeer Farm, since once upon a time her grandfather had owned the herd with Theo Adler.

"Ellie!" Her brother, Jamie, gave her a big hug.

She was then handed off to her older brother, Owen, who was close in age to Liam. It was good to see them.

"How's Albuquerque?" she asked Owen. He was at UNM getting an MBA.

He shrugged. "The same. I can't believe you've come back. You were our world traveler."

"Even world travelers get tired." She leaned close and said in a low voice, "You'll be home for good soon, too. You've gotta help dad with the Thatcher portfolio."

"I know. Is it true that Liam Adler is now running the Adler empire?"

"Yes, I guess so." She feigned a nonchalance she wasn't feeling, because in the last hour she'd come to realize that Liam Adler was a huge problem for her. She liked him. Like *really* liked him. Man, this was going to make living in town a bear.

She grabbed a saltine and a slice of cheddar cheese from the hors d'oeuvre plate on the kitchen island and started munching. Two hours with the magnificent Lumi—and the magnificent Liam—and she was famished.

"Slow down, El," Owen admonished. "You'll ruin your dinner. I have it on good authority that Grandma made her famous lasagna."

Ellie groaned with happiness. Her grandmother was a testament to her Italian heritage. Then she did a quick scan of those present. "Where's Bella?"

Owen dug a cracker into a bowl of pimento and shrugged as he popped it into his mouth. "Mason said she had a date."

Since Mason, their cousin and Bella's brother, was currently chatting with Ellie's dad, she was forced to pump Owen for more information.

"Did he say with who?" she asked. It was incomprehensible that Bella would have such a rebellious streak in her. It went against the fabric of her personality.

"No. And why don't you know? You two were always like conjoined twins."

"Maybe it's just casual," she said, more to herself. "Not serious. Not worth talking about. Yeah, that's probably it." Was she talking about Liam now?

Owen gave her a funny look, which she ignored.

Her dad stepped away from Mason and gave her a hug, and said quietly, "Your mother told me about the dog. I might have a solution for you."

"Really?" Ellie brightened.

"I know you want to move out. I've got a friend who owns a condo down by the creek. His tenant had to break the lease suddenly, so if you want it, he'll have it ready to move into before Christmas. And he'll let you have a dog."

"That's fantastic!"

"We can see it in a few days, if you like."

"Yes, absolutely. Thanks, Dad." She gave him another hug.

While they all waited for the piping-hot lasagna to cool, Ellie got Grandpa Adam to join her in the living room. She had the journal on her lap.

"I've been in the mountains recently taking photos," she said, "and I found an old, abandoned cabin. I think it was used by Charlie Thatcher and Henry Adler in the late 1800's. I found this journal, and it was written by Eleonoora Thatcher."

She'd decided not to mention that Liam had been with her, or that he had been the one to find the journal. She didn't want to aggravate her grandfather over Theo Adler's idea that Ellie needed to have guardianship while in the mountains.

"Is that so?" He took the book from her.

"It's written in Finnish, but I've been able to translate some of the beginning."

"You speak the language?" he asked.

"A little. I learned last year when I lived in Finland. Mom told me you also speak it."

"It's been a long time." He pointed at the journal. "Granny taught me."

"What was she like?"

"Quiet. Always outdoors. She'd come with her father to deliver a herd of reindeer and she married my great-grandfather, Charlie. But she told me once that Henry Adler had wanted to court her."

"You're kidding." What was it about Thatcher and Adler men fighting over the same woman? But she didn't say it aloud since her own grandfather had stolen Theo Adler's girl so many years ago.

Adam gave a wry chuckle. "I guess the apple doesn't fall too far from the tree."

Ellie would admonish her grandfather over stealing Theo's girl, except if he hadn't then Ellie wouldn't be sitting here today.

"Eleonoora wrote about a large female reindeer. Do you think this was the original Vaadin?"

"Are you caught up in that nonsense too, Ellie?"

"But you saw the Vaadin with grandma. Eustace told me."

"Granny did speak of the Arctic reindeer, but I've never seen them," her grandfather said. "And I sometimes wondered if she was just telling stories to amuse me."

"Was she some type of shaman?"

"I'm not sure. Why do you ask?"

"Just some references in her journal. I thought it might have something to do with the reindeer."

"She had a unique relationship with animals," he said. "She told me once that instead of going back to Finland she'd stayed because of Charlie, but also for the reindeer."

"But there were reindeer in Finland."

"She did say that the ones she and her father had brought were special."

"Would you be able to translate some of her words for me?" she asked.

"I'm afraid I'm a bit out of practice. There must be a reason you found the journal. Perhaps she's reaching out across time to you. Maybe she wants you to read it."

Eleven

The following morning, Ellie drove to Eustace's cabin. She'd called first and he'd agreed as long as she brought a bribe. She parked and grabbed the box of muffins—an assortment since she wasn't sure what Eustace liked—that she'd picked up at Bella's Bakery and carefully navigated the snow-covered walkway to his front door. The sun was shining and there was a crispness to the air. It was bright and early, but she'd already planned to take the morning off from her studio to spend time in the mountains continuing her search for the reindeer now that the snowfall had abated. And maybe she'd see the Vaadin. Or maybe she was avoiding Liam when he arrived at the office.

She glanced around at the forest and the rays of light hitting the snow and felt rejuvenated.

She'd tried to call Bella last night to pump her for info about her date, but there'd been no answer, and Ellie had finally gone to sleep after she'd read Eleonoora's journal late into the night. That morning at the bakery Bella had been quite busy and her mother was there helping, so

Ellie didn't ask about it, instead saying they should talk later.

Ellie knocked on the door. Eustace swung it open and Lilja greeted her with unabashed joy.

"Hi, sweetheart!"

"She really seems to like you."

"The feeling is mutual." Ellie showered attention on the girl. "I can take her but not for another week when I'll be getting my own place. Can you keep her until then? I do come bearing your bribe." She handed the muffins to him, holding them high to avoid Lilja's hyper-interest in the food.

"Blueberry?"

"Absolutely."

"Then I'll keep crazy girl for another week. Come inside and I'll get some tea going."

She followed him into the kitchen, and in an amiable silence they worked together—she found two small plates in the cupboard and put a muffin on each while Eustace made tea from already heated water. When Ellie sat, Lilja lay at her feet.

"I have something to show you." She pulled a folder from her bag and handed it to him. "I present to you the Vaadin."

He pulled on a pair of reading glasses and inspected the photo.

"Well?" she prompted.

"She's beautiful. Where did you see her?"

"Last night at the Adler Reindeer Farm. Liam's father had her shipped from Finland. He'd planned it before his death."

"That was very thoughtful of him." Eustace set the picture aside and cut his muffin into quarters with a knife.

"Does this count?" she asked.

"Do *you* think it counts?" He ate a slice of muffin.

She wanted it to, because after finding Eleonoora's abandoned cabin a strong desire to have ownership of it had overtaken her. And for that she needed her grandfather to buy Eustace's property, and then to convince him to somehow sell the cabin to her. Since she had little money, perhaps he would hold the mortgage. She really should have spoken to Grandpa Adam about it all last night, but the timing hadn't seemed right.

But Eustace's question filled the air, the answer already ringing in her bones.

"No," she admitted. "How are you so sure? The Vaadin you saw is long dead by now."

"You have to see with something other than your eyes. The reindeer can see beyond what we can. To see like they do, you must use your other senses."

"But you told us to take a photo."

He dusted crumbs from his hands and wiped his mouth with a paper napkin decorated with poinsettias. "I told you what you wanted to hear. Do you always do what you're told?"

That brought Ellie up short. The time she'd spent in Finland had been filled with long days and hard work, but also awe, eerie coincidences, and a fine-tuning of her intuition. But since coming home, she seemed to have forgotten it.

"Trust your instincts, Ellie," Eustace said. "You'll know the Vaadin when you see it."

Ellie tamped down her frustration, but she couldn't help but ask, "Why are Mark Osborn and Jennifer Dixon included in this? Wouldn't it make sense that a Thatcher or an Adler should have your land? Aren't they the ones who gave it to your ancestors in the first place?"

Eustace took a sip of his tea and settled back into his

chair, the wood creaking in protest. "That part is true. But the Osborns and the Dixons were also here in the 1880's."

"They were?"

"Don't be so surprised. People often return to places that call to them, although they no longer know why. But on some level, they're still connected to the land."

Jennifer had never mentioned that her family ties went that far back in the area. Maybe she didn't know.

"So you're saying that any one of us is entitled to your land based on the mythology of a female reindeer from Finland."

He shrugged. "That's what I feel in my bones."

Something about the bones nagged at her but she couldn't say what.

"Can I ask a favor?" Ellie said. "Liam and I found an old cabin the last time we were here that had been used by Eleonoora Thatcher at one time."

"I know it."

"Well, Liam had a survey done and it's on your property."

"I could've told you that. All you had to do was ask."

"Sorry," she said. "There were some photos and a journal that belonged to our families. I hope you don't mind, but I took them."

"That sounds fair. You know," he said thoughtfully. "I've seen deer tracks quite frequently up there. You should consider using it as a home base." Then he added, "For your photos, of course."

Ellie had been wondering the same thing. "I'd like that. You don't mind if I clean the place up a bit?"

"Suit yourself."

"Thanks." She stood and Lilja jumped to her feet, staring up at her. "I guess I should be heading out."

"Why don't you take her with you," Eustace suggested.

"How do you know I'm going into the woods?"

Eustace smiled. "Lucky guess."

She looked into the dog's brown eyes, feeling a surge of love. "I'll bring her back when I'm done."

Eustace nodded and followed them to the front door. While Ellie donned her winter gear, he put a fleece dog sweater on Lilja. "A gift from Mark's parents."

Ellie mentally made a note to bring a gift for Lilja the next time she visited.

"Thank you for the muffins. And here's a tip, just for you, Ellie."

Standing on the porch, he looked like a painting of an old man watching from his warm, cozy cabin, a sparkle in his gaze. Santa Claus.

"Yuletide is a special time, a time between time. When my wife and I saw the Vaadin, it was then. When your grandparents did, it was also during that period."

Ellie racked her brain. What were the exact dates of Yule? Hadn't she learned it while in Finland?

"It has something to do with the Solstice?" she asked.

Eustace nodded. "December 20 to December 31."

With a smile, he closed the door.

Today was December 17.

ELLIE LOST track of time as she cleaned the abandoned cabin, Lilja going in and out the front door, which Ellie left open to help disperse the dust. It was satisfying to tidy up the place. There were no more journals from Eleonoora, but Ellie found additional books all in Finnish. Her great-great grandmother had definitely spent time here. The photos she'd found earlier seemed to indicate that Charlie Thatcher and Henry Adler had been here as well. Her dad had confirmed the identities of both men.

The physical labor of cleaning was a welcome outlet for her growing frustration when it came to Liam. And when she was done here, she'd explore the woods in search of reindeer. She really needed to stay focused on her main agenda—supporting her photography by getting pictures for the magazine job.

Her cellphone rang, playing a rousing rendition of "Sleigh Bells," and she was surprised the cell tower signal was good out here, considering the remoteness, while also experiencing a leap in her pulse. Maybe it was Liam.

But it was Bella.

"Hi, Ellie. Have you been trying to get a hold of me?"

"Yes! Can you talk? Are you alone?"

"Yes. I'm on a break and my mom is out cleaning tables."

Ellie didn't waste any time cutting to the chase. "Did you go out with Ryan Adler last night?"

The silence on the other end was confirmation enough.

"How do you know about that?" Bella finally asked, her voice barely above a whisper.

"Liam."

"He knows?"

"I think he suspected. But it turns out he was right! Why didn't you say anything?"

A rhetorical question if there ever was one. Bella hadn't told anyone, least of all Ellie, because she didn't want anyone to know.

"I thought you didn't like Adlers," Ellie accused.

"I didn't. But … well … Ryan is different."

Ellie's mouth hung open in shock. Then she laughed. "You're a traitor, Bella."

"I am not! I tried to avoid him. Really, I did."

Bella was smitten. Ellie could hear it in her cousin's voice. "How long have you liked him?"

More hesitation, and then a quiet, "A while."

How long have I liked Liam? A while too.

"What did you do last night?" Ellie asked.

"He took me to Durango."

"That's a long drive." At least two hours if the roads are clear and the weather is good. "You two really didn't want to be seen."

"There was no reason to cause a commotion. I mean, what if this doesn't work out?"

"Did he kiss you?"

Another pause. Another confirmation.

"Do you like him, Bells? I mean do you really, really like him?"

No hesitation. "Yes."

"Then I'm happy for you. It's gonna be tricky though."

"I know. Don't say anything yet, okay? No reason to get everyone all upset."

"No problem," Ellie said.

"Hey, why aren't you in your studio today?"

"I don't have an influx of customers like you. I've posted my website on the door so anyone can reach me that way. Besides, I wanted to explore that abandoned cabin I told you about. And try to get more photos out here."

"Maybe you shouldn't be up there alone."

"It's okay. I've got Eustace's dog with me."

"Eustace has a dog?" Bella asked.

"And she's soon to be mine. He's given her to me."

"Aww, that's wonderful. I can't wait to meet her."

❄

Ellie's studio had been closed when Liam arrived this morning. Now it was just past noon, and still no sign of her, so he headed to Bella's to grab a sandwich hoping she was there. On the way, he ran into Jennifer.

"Mind if I join you for lunch?" she asked when she realized where he was headed.

He couldn't think of a good reason to say no. "Sure."

They ordered their food and Liam wanted to ask Bella about Ellie's whereabouts, but the bakery was too busy for chatting. He could, of course, simply call Ellie, but aside from asking her on a date outright, he had no other reason to phone her. And he wasn't sure if Ellie would be receptive to an outright date.

Ryan had remained tight-lipped at the office about his evening with Bella, so Liam couldn't tell if it had gone well or if it had crashed and burned. However, Ryan's mood had been fairly upbeat, so Liam took that as a good sign that a Thatcher might return the affections of an Adler.

"It's nice to see you again," Jennifer said once they were at a table, one she'd had to grab quickly when the previous occupants had stood. She removed her scarf and hat. "It's hard to believe how long it's been. Ten years? Gosh, we were just kids back then."

"It's been a long time," he agreed.

Bella delivered their food, and Liam took a bite of his turkey, stuffing, and cranberry sandwich. It was fast becoming his favorite food item.

Jennifer mixed dressing into her salad, and said, "I can't help but think it's fate that we both ended up back in Barstow at the same time."

Liam took another bite of his sandwich, unsure how to reply. Did she want another chance at dating him? Back then, they'd both been young, and it had been very casual. She hadn't lived in town, and distance had easily dissolved any interest between them. There had been no hard feelings. At least, not on his side.

He wiped his fingers with a napkin and said, "Is there something I'm missing here? Are you upset about the way we ended things?"

"Oh no, of course not. I just can't help but wonder how it might've been if we'd stayed together, if we'd gotten more serious."

Uh oh. Time to set things right. "I appreciate the nostalgia, but I'm not …."

"You have a girlfriend?"

"No, but there is someone. It's just early yet with her."

"Oh, of course. I understand." But her embarrassment was readily apparent as she plastered a pained smile on her face.

Liam felt like a heel. He'd been friendly with Jennifer since reconnecting again, but he'd most definitely not been flirting with her.

"Maybe under different circumstances," he said.

Bella came to their table, her apron sporting coffee stains. "I'm sorry to interrupt, but Ellie is up at that old cabin you both found, and she's alone. Well, apparently there's a dog, but I'm worried about her."

Liam was about to offer to drive up there, but Jennifer jumped in. "I'm going to the Christmas Village. I can check on her."

"That would be great," Bella said. "Can I get either of you anything? A scone, maybe? On the house?"

Jennifer stood and scooped up her belongings. "No, I'm good. I need to get going, but I'll check in on Ellie." She waved goodbye and was quickly gone.

"What did you say to her?" Bella's tone was part baffled and part accusatory.

"Why do you think I said something?"

"She looked like she was trying to get away from you. Didn't you two date a long time ago?"

"That's ancient history. What's going on with you and Ryan?"

"Shhh." She moved to block his view of her mother behind the counter. "Can you not gossip about us?" she added in a whisper.

"I'm not gossiping, Bella. I'm just a concerned brother. Try not to break his heart."

That seemed to take Bella by surprise. "I won't," she said softly. "I need to get back to work, but I'll get you that scone."

She returned with a bag and handed it to him. "I wasn't sure what you like, so I gave you a plain one and an iced cranberry."

"Thank you."

"Well, you *are* Ryan's brother, so I suppose that doesn't make you all bad."

"I think that's the nicest thing you've ever said to me."

She made a face then quickly recovered her composure. Liam grinned and left the bakery.

Twelve

Lilja started barking, and Ellie set down the rag she'd been using to clean the small, south-facing window and went outside to see what the ruckus was all about.

Jennifer was trudging toward the cabin.

Ellie waved hello. "How'd you find me?"

Jennifer stepped onto the porch, trying to catch her breath. "Bella wanted me to check on you. Eustace told me how to find the place. I had no idea this was here."

"I wish I could offer you a hot drink, but how about a tour? It'll take about thirty seconds."

Jennifer smiled and followed Ellie inside. After taking in the one-room dwelling, she said, "I'm impressed. This should be classified a historical building."

"I was thinking the same. Did you know there were Dixons here back in the 1800's?"

"I know a little. I guess that's why my parents always liked it here."

Ellie looked around the place, looking much better after her morning of tender loving care. "Whoever gets

Eustace's land will need to do something about this place," she said.

"This is his land?"

Ellie nodded, hands on hips. That's when she noticed the frown lines around Jennifer's mouth. "Is everything all right?"

"Yeah, sure. Well, no. I'm feeling a bit foolish."

"About what?"

"I made a play for Liam."

Oh. Ellie's stomach dropped. "You don't have to talk about it, if you don't want to."

But Jennifer plowed forward. "He let me down, gently I might add. I guess I was silly for thinking maybe there was still something there. He's interested in someone else."

Ellie's spine straightened as if zapped by electricity. "Who?" So much for staying neutral.

"I don't know. I didn't ask. I'm assuming it's someone from Pennsylvania."

Oh. Yes, that made sense. No wonder he was unhappy being forced to come home and run the family business. And his interest in Ellie? Clearly it had all been in her head.

"Are you sure you don't want to go to the ball with my brother?" Jen asked. "If you're with Liam, this mysterious girlfriend might show up and not be happy with your friend status."

Oh. Clearly, she needed to ditch the pretend date with Liam.

"Good point," Ellie said. "But I'll be all right."

"Well, I need to go. I've got a pile of paperwork at the Village waiting for me. Stay safe up here." Then she turned back. "Oh, and if by chance you see this elusive Vaadin, will you give me a call? Maybe if us girls stick together, I can still manage to make a bit of money from Eustace's land. I'd cut you in."

"Thanks." But the last thing Ellie was looking to do was make a profit off Eustace.

With Jennifer gone, Ellie quietly licked her wounded pride over thinking Liam had felt anything for her beyond polite acquaintance and grabbed her pack. She secured the cabin, then took off for the forest, looking forward to physical activity to burn off her frustration, Lilja at her heels. That's when she noticed the tracks off to the side. The hoofprints were large, and Ellie was certain they belonged to reindeer.

It would be worthwhile spending more time here. If she brought an air mattress and a sleeping bag, wood for the cast iron stove, snacks, and water, then she could stay for hours, even overnight. A glance at Lilja, the dog's nose to the slushy snow as she inspected the tracks on a path that looked like figure eights, Ellie decided she'd bring a dog bed, dog food, and a water dish for the mutt as well.

She and Lilja hiked for almost two hours, but came up with nothing, although Ellie had gotten quite a few excellent photos of the lab. Soon to be her lab.

With a sigh, Ellie knew she would need to return to the Adler Reindeer Farm. She'd ask Mick if she could see Lumi, especially during the day. The photos would have better light, and surely Liam would be working and not at the farm.

After returning Lilja to Eustace, Ellie entered her parents' house close to six p.m.

Her mom was making cookies in the kitchen. "Hi, Ellie. Dinner is simple tonight." She nodded at the opposite counter. "Pizza."

Ellie grabbed a plate and two slices of pepperoni, and

a glass of ice water, then sat at the kitchen table. Her long day had left her hungry, and she quickly inhaled the food.

Then she went to her mother and gave her a hug from behind, engulfing her since Ellie was taller.

"What's this?" her mom said.

"I just wanted to tell you I love you, and that I'm so glad the breast biopsy was negative."

"Me too, sweetie."

For a moment, Ellie clung to her mother, feeling so much gratitude. Then she peeked over her mom's shoulder at the cookies cooling on the racks spread on every open countertop.

"Which ones can I eat?" she asked.

"The snickerdoodles."

Ellie pointed at the ones with icing. "What about these?"

"Those are gingerbread oatmeal. You may have *only* one."

After one more hug for her mom, Ellie collected her booty onto a plate, poured herself a glass of milk, and went back to the table. "These are delicious, Mom."

"Thank you."

"Where's Dad and the boys?"

"They said they were going Christmas shopping, if you can believe it. Any reindeer sightings?"

"No. But the Adlers got a special delivery yesterday, and Liam invited me to be there for it. It was a new reindeer for the farm, shipped all the way from Finland."

"You always wanted to be an Adler," her mother murmured as she squeezed icing onto her latest batch of sugar cookies.

Ellie collected the cookie crumbs on her plate with her index finger then nibbled them off. "What are you saying?"

"When you were young you would bemoan the fact

that the Adler had the reindeer, and we didn't. You even confronted Grandpa Adam about it once."

"I did?" That memory was lost to Ellie.

Her mother laughed. "You told him it wasn't fair that the Adler boys got to take care of Santa's reindeer. That they were all buttheads and didn't deserve such a special assignment. In your defense, those Adler boys did get into trouble, but then so did your brothers."

"You knew about all of them hanging out?"

"Of course. Mothers talk. We kept each other posted."

Ellie frowned. Did her mother know that she had a crush on Liam Adler? A crush that was going nowhere? "Did you ever punish Jamie and Owen for running around with them?"

"Only when they did something wrong. But no, not specifically for being with the Adler boys."

Ellie's cellphone buzzed in her pocket. She pulled it out and saw a text from Liam.

Want to see Lumi tonight?

Yes. And you. Damn her traitorous heart.

She glanced at her mom to see if she knew about the text, but Anna Thatcher was busy stirring a pan of chocolate that she'd just melted.

Her mom looked up. "What are you smiling at?"

"You."

"What do you want?" her mom asked, suspicion in her voice.

"Nothing. Well, maybe a few cookies? I'm going to head over to the Reindeer Farm."

"Now?"

"I've got to make sure those Adler boys take care of Santa's reindeer."

❄

Ellie arrived forty-five minutes after Liam had texted her.

"Are you planning to photograph Lumi's individual hairs?" he asked, looking at the large camera and even larger lens suspended from a strap crosswise on her body.

"Funny," she said in a deadpan voice. "I wasn't sure where'd you have her and how close I could get. I've got a smaller lens, too." She handed him a festive tin. "From my mom."

He popped the lid. Homemade cookies. "These look amazing. Please tell her thank you. That is, if you want her to know where you've been."

"I told her. Apparently, she's known about your escapades with my brothers for years. There seems to be no reason to hide our association." She walked past him to the corral where Lumi was on display for night visitors to the farm, although it was almost closing time.

She started taking photos as Liam ate two snowball cookies. He went inside the barn and retrieved the two cups of hot chocolate he'd gotten from the concession stand, then returned to Ellie's side.

She was so focused on Lumi, who admittedly was quite striking—not only the immense height of her but the breadth of her antlers—that when he gently nudged Ellie with his elbow, she jumped in surprise, staring at the cup in his hand.

"Is that for me?"

"Yes."

But she didn't take it. Instead, she watched it like he was offering a potion of hemlock.

"It's not going to bite you," he said. "You brought me cookies. Can't I at least offer you something to drink?"

"Yeah, sure. Thanks." She took the beverage and then turned back to Lumi.

There seemed to be a frostiness in the air that had nothing to do with the weather. He had a sneaking suspicion what it might be.

"Did you see Jennifer Dixon today?" he asked.

"Yes. I was at the old cabin, and she stopped by."

"I suppose you two talk."

"That's generally what people do when in each other's company." She fiddled with the settings on her camera and then snapped a few more photos. She wasn't using a flash, which probably explained why Lumi approached them, going straight to Ellie.

The large female stopped before them, white puffs of air coming from her nostrils. For a long moment, the two females watched each other, and Liam felt like an interloper.

Ellie reached out her hand, and Liam bit back a comment. According to Mick, the reindeer had been standoffish today, so no one had really handled her, and they certainly hadn't been petting her. It was unclear whether they could let customers interact with Lumi beyond seeing her from afar. Liam didn't profess to know much about the animals—he'd never been that interested in the farm growing up—but Ellie had worked here years ago, and her love of reindeer was still evident.

Ellie extended her arm through the fence slats, her palm forward, and Lumi pushed her nose against it. Their affinity for one another was palpable. Almost magical.

"Maybe you should work here again," he said quietly.

"Don't tempt me." But her focus remained on Lumi.

"Unfortunately, the farm isn't our biggest money-maker. Over the last few years, it's been steadily losing money."

Now she met his gaze. "Are you thinking of getting rid of it?" The concern on her face was fierce and immediate.

"No. But I'm not sure what will happen in the future."

"If you want to sell, maybe the Thatchers could buy it. Ever since I was a little girl, I've wished that we had the farm."

"Are you making me an offer?" he asked.

"Maybe." She looked back at Lumi, the love in her eyes clear as day, even in the waning light. "It was like your family had an in with Santa every year. I was deeply envious. By the way, Eustace doesn't accept Lumi as the Vaadin."

"It was worth a try. Listen, about Jennifer."

Ellie shook her head, a bit too vigorously. "You don't have to explain anything to me." She pulled her hand back and took a sip of her hot chocolate.

Liam's goal tonight had been clear—he would invite Ellie over so they could hang out casually, and then he'd invite her to dinner the next day. But now he felt a bit confused. What had Jennifer said? Was Ellie mad? He was hesitant about how to proceed, worried that he didn't quite understand the playing field and might inadvertently blow his chance.

They watched Lumi with a charged silence between them.

What the hell. "Ellie, would you have dinner with me Friday night?"

Her brow furrowed. "At your grandfather's house? No offense, Liam, but I've already done that, and I don't think it was good for his blood pressure."

"No, I mean just with me."

"Why?"

This wasn't going well. "I would like to take you on a date."

"What about your girlfriend in Pennsylvania?"

Huh? "I don't have a girlfriend, there or here."

"Oh." She took another sip, her forehead marred with worry lines.

Disappointment pressed in on him. He'd really thought she liked him. "You can just say no if you don't want to go."

"It's not that." Her worried face smoothed into bashfulness. "Are you sure about this? Bella and Ryan are already proving the difficulties involved in a Thatcher and an Adler trying to be … friends. Or … friendly. Not that we're friendly."

Liam felt the tension leave his body that he hadn't even been aware he was carrying until it was gone. Relief—and happiness—replaced it. Ellie Thatcher liked him.

"And then there's Jennifer," she added.

"She was a long time ago," he said. "I have no interest in rekindling anything with her."

A tiny smile crept to her mouth. "You know this won't run smoothly."

"When has anything ever been easy between us?"

That extracted a laugh from her, a most magical sound.

Thirteen

On Thursday, Ellie spent the day in the mountains at the old cabin with Lilja. She'd brought the dog a big chew bone and that had kept her busy while Ellie had managed to see several of the wild reindeer and get photos. On Friday, Ellie went into her studio because she had two bookings for Christmas photos—one with older children who were a bit grouchy about getting dressed up, so she'd been hard-pressed to get decent shots, and the other involved a baby and a goofy golden retriever which had almost been harder to handle than thc morose teens. By the time she was finished, she was exhausted and having been so busy, she had missed seeing Liam come or go from his upstairs office. Probably a blessing. Better that she hadn't had time to think about the coming evening. But she did have a few questions, so she should probably call him. She texted instead, not wanting to seem too eager.

Hi. Should I meet you tonight?

His response came ten agonizing minutes later.

No. I'll pick you up.

But she lived with her parents, and he lived with his grandparents.

Okay. I'll be at my studio, so pick me up here. I'll be working late.

Not entirely true, but it would be easier this way. No unnecessary family questions. She glanced at her watch.

What time?

I'll be by at six. I'm not at the office today.

That explained why she hadn't seen him all day.

Are we going to Durango?

Why Durango?

It's where Ryan took Bella the other night. Incognito.

She added a laughing emoji.

Sly. But no. I'm taking you to The Caribou Inn.

What? It was smack in the center of Reindeer Pass.

Do you have a death wish?

We'll be off the radar.

She wasn't so sure about that, but she didn't want to begin the evening with her nagging him, so she let it go. Another glance at her watch. She had enough time to run home and get a change of clothes, something understated so no one would notice her. But The Caribou Inn was a bit fancy and normally she would dress up. Shc grabbed her keys, locked up the studio, and jumped in her car. She needed as much time as possible to figure out what to wear on her date with Liam Adler.

LIAM PULLED up to Ellie's photography studio, but before he could get out of the car, she was outside, her back to him as she locked the door. She shuffled quickly into his SUV, her legs clad in dark stockings and her feet in black heels. He tried not to stare.

"I'm surprised you're not wearing a costume," he teased, to distract himself from the alluring view she presented. He especially liked that her hair was down.

"My reindeer ensemble is in storage." She clicked into her seatbelt. "Are you sure about this?"

Was she referring to dinner together or simply being together?

"I'm sure." To both. Was it only a few weeks ago that he'd thought Ryan was crazy for pursuing Bella?

"You look nice," he added. She smelled nice too, a fruity scent with an underlying hint of spice. A bit like Ellie herself.

"Thanks."

He adjusted the heat and then eased the vehicle onto the road.

"So why The Caribou Inn?" she asked.

"I wanted to take you some place nice. Would you rather we eat in the old cabin on Eustace's property?"

"It's private, if not cold. I've cleaned it up and added a few amenities so I can hang out for long periods."

"The girl who trespasses."

She scoffed. "Your grandfather gave me permission, as did Eustace."

"So you're planning to squat and refuse to leave?"

He turned onto the main road that connected Barstow to Reindeer Pass. Darkness was nearly upon them, and Christmas lights sparkled as they passed houses tucked back off the highway.

"Hah, maybe. Is your mother ready for the ball tomorrow?"

"I think so. She's got several ladies in town helping, and they took care of things during and after my dad's funeral, but I think working on it has helped her stay busy."

"Probably a good thing. How are you doing?" Her tone was sincere.

"I haven't lived here for some time, so I didn't see my dad on a daily basis. There are times when I imagine he's still here, and I expect him to take a seat at the dinner table with the rest of us. And then I remember …. Honestly, it doesn't seem real."

"I'm sure Christmas will be difficult for you all."

"I know our grandfathers don't get along, but Theo has been more ornery than usual. I think it's because of Dad."

"I'm sure you're right."

He pulled into the parking lot of The Caribou Inn and spent several minutes looking for a spot.

"It looks busy," she murmured.

"I have a reservation. And to ease your mind, it's a private room. It looks like I'm going to have to park across the street. I'll drop you at the entrance, so you don't have to walk."

He stopped the vehicle. A young man opened the passenger door and helped Ellie out.

"I'll just be a few minutes," he said. "Go on inside. The reservation is under Adler."

The wind had picked up. Ellie nodded, clutching her wool coat together, and ran inside.

It was another ten minutes before Liam entered the restaurant.

As SOON AS THE MAÎTRE D' guided Ellie to a table that was *not* in a private room, her panic mode activated. Theo and Charlotte Adler were speaking to their waiter as they cast their attention on the menus in their hands.

Ellie grabbed the maître d's arm. "There's been a mix-up," she whispered frantically. "This isn't my table."

Pulling hard, she swung the man around and hustled him back to the front of the restaurant before Liam's grandparents could see her.

"Ellie?"

She spun to the familiar voice coming from her left. "Mom?"

"What are you doing here?" Her mother stepped closer, looking pretty in a silver sheath and black velvet pants.

"I'm … meeting someone."

Her mother's eyes widened in surprise. "Are you on a date?"

"What? No! Is Dad here?" Ellie began scanning behind her mother.

"Yes. He surprised me at the last minute. It's a Christmas date. That man still has some romance in him. Why don't you join us?"

"No, no. I'm not going to intrude on your special evening. I'm just meeting a friend."

"Who?"

Liam would make an appearance at any moment. She

needed to think fast, but her mind went blank. And then Bella entered the restaurant, wearing a cute little black dress with a sparkling Christmas Rudolph brooch.

"Bella!" Ella exclaimed.

"Why are you referring to Bella as your friend?" her mother asked.

"Because she is my friend." Ella rushed up to her cousin and whispered quickly, "Please cover for me." She spun around as her mother stepped closer.

"Girls, you look so beautiful," Ellie's mom exclaimed. "You both really should dine with us."

"No," Ellie cut in. "Bella and I were looking forward to some girl time. Just us. You know how it is."

Her mother looked confused. "I suppose. All right. Well, we should drive you both home. The roads will be icy. We'll look for you when we're finished with supper." She spun on her heel before either of them could respond.

"What's going on?" Bella asked.

Liam walked inside and smiled.

A small gasp escaped Bella. "Are you on a date?"

Ellie pressed her lips together, still slick from the pale pink lipstick she'd applied earlier. "I … uh."

She was saved from a reply when Ryan appeared in the waiting area.

Ellie looked at Bella. "This is awfully public for you two."

"Why did you lie to your mother about us having dinner together?" Bella countered.

"Ellie, did you check in?" Liam asked.

She cast an exasperated look at him, and he responded with a laugh.

Ellie linked her arm with Bella's and dragged her toward their dates. "Your grandparents are here. The maître d' almost sat me at their table. There's too many

Adlers here." Then she added, "And my parents are here too."

"I didn't think we'd be outed so soon," Ryan said, but he shrugged.

"What are you saying?" Ellie demanded in a fierce whisper. "This is going to ruin Christmas for all of them. There's no reason for that." And then her heart went into triple beats. "Oh no." Through the entrance window, she saw *her* grandparents, and they were about to walk in. "Scatter!"

She and Bella ran to the ladies' room. Once inside, Bella's hand went to her chest as she tried to catch her breath. "I told Ryan we should've gone to Durango again." Then Bella honed in on Ellie. "Why didn't you tell me about you and Liam?"

"Because there is no me and Liam. This is our first dinner. I have no idea where this is going. Just like you and Ryan."

Suddenly they both burst out laughing and fell into the stuffed chairs in the ladies lounge.

"Who knew the Adler boys were so irresistible?" Bella said.

While Ryan didn't catch Ellie's eye, there was no debating Liam's magnetism.

"We should leave, I suppose," Ellie said. "Go eat at that burger joint in Barstow."

"It might be okay. Ryan said he booked a private room."

"Liam did the same."

"We just have to make sure we don't enter or leave the room with them, that's all." Bella stood, wobbling a bit in her heels.

Ellie rose to her feet as well. "You look really nice,

Bells." She fluffed her cousin's hair. "You must really like him."

Bella became serious. "I do. If you and Liam are serious too, then you two could tell the families first, lessening the shock of me and Ryan."

"Nice try. If this works out, I'm not planning to tell Grandpa Adam until my tenth wedding anniversary, and Liam and I have three kids."

They laughed again.

"All right," Bella said. "Enough hiding in here. Let's go."

They squared their shoulders as *Rudolph the Red-Nosed Reindeer* played over the lounge speakers.

They furtively walked the hallway back to the entrance, then each took turns peeking around corners. Since Liam and Ryan were gone, they were forced to ask the front desk where they had gone. Luckily the private nooks weren't far from each other, and Ellie slipped into the one occupied by Liam as Bella disappeared into hers.

Liam sat at the table, menu in hand. "I was beginning to think I was going to eat alone."

"You sure know how to show a girl a stressful night."

He stood and pulled out her chair, scooting it in as she sat.

"Thank you," she said.

"I ordered you a glass of wine. I wasn't sure what you like, so there's a red and a white. I'll drink whichever one you don't want."

She smiled, finally relaxing. "I'll take both."

Fourteen

Liam was glad to finally have Ellie at the table, although it had been a bit dicey there for a few minutes. He'd caught sight of his grandparents in the main dining room and had the host show him to his table immediately, even though his date had been holed up in the ladies' restroom.

The intimate table for two decorated with pinecones and holly lent a romantic atmosphere. He'd wanted to impress his date which was why he'd gambled on the location, one of the nicest establishments within fifty miles.

The waiter returned and Ellie quickly scanned the menu and ordered, so Liam scrambled to choose his entrée as well. She was moving things along.

Ellie grabbed a hot roll from the breadbasket, sliced it in half, and added a generous portion of butter before consuming it in record time.

"I didn't realize how hungry I was," she said with a laugh. "I guess I've been a little nervous about tonight and I didn't eat much all day."

He'd had a bout of nerves as well. "Then you'd better eat before you drink that wine."

"My thoughts exactly. Everyone and their neighbor is here tonight." She took a sip of the chardonnay and offered the other glass to him.

"Maybe I should've taken you to Durango," he said, accepting the red and taking a drink.

"Next time?" Merriment danced in her eyes, the thread of attraction winding around them.

He nodded, glad she wanted to do this again, despite the unknown territory they were both about to enter. But she'd always held his attention in a unique way.

She'd been both endearing and maddening as a child, and then quietly impressive in her teens. The first tug of romantic attraction had been five years ago at the Reindeer Ball when his logical reason for protecting her from Mark Osborn's advances had been born out of a brotherly feeling, but in truth had been entangled with something a bit more primal. But she'd been on the cusp of breaking into adulthood, and he'd been in his phase of not being tied down to Reindeer Pass, so he'd chalked it up to a cursory fascination and tucked it into his memory bank.

But Ellie Thatcher wasn't something to be relegated to his past. That was obvious now. He'd been a fool to think he could simply be her friend when even that was frowned upon by their families.

The salads arrived, and as they began eating, Liam said, "I'm still surprised you came back to Reindeer Pass." *But happy you did.*

"I suppose a few years ago it wouldn't have been a choice I'd make, but my mom had a health scare."

"I'm sorry. I didn't know."

"She's okay now, but I didn't want to be so far away anymore."

The waiter returned and topped off their water glasses. "Your dinner will be out shortly," he said and left.

"I guess I envy you," Liam said.

She popped a cherry tomato in her mouth, chewed thoughtfully, then said, "You wouldn't have come back, would you, if you hadn't had to?"

No reason to hide the truth. "No."

A shadow of disappointment crossed her face. "What's in Pennsylvania that you miss so much?"

Damn. She had him. "Nothing," he answered a bit sheepishly. "I guess I thought my life was there, not here. Anywhere but here, I suppose."

A server brought their entrees—pasta for her and a filet for him.

"Why do you dislike Reindeer Pass so much?" She ate a piece of ravioli. "Wow. This is good."

"I don't dislike it." He added sour cream and chives to his baked potato. "It just always felt small, and I wanted something bigger."

"Me, too. But I think being far from home is overrated. We think we need distance from our families, but the truth is, the only thing that matters *are* our families."

"True." He took a bite of his filet and it all but melted in his mouth. "You should try this." He cut a piece for her, and her distracting lips took it directly from his fork.

"You should try mine." She offered up a ravioli on her fork, and he accepted it, feeling the undercurrent of hunger between them that had nothing to do with food.

"I like it," he said.

Color rose in her cheeks, and she returned her attention to her meal. "Do you wish you had spent more time with your dad?" she asked.

"Yeah. You always think you have more time than you do. How's it going with Eleonoora's journal?"

"Well, this might sound silly, but I think there was a pact made between Charlie Thatcher and Henry Adler. A blessing of some kind via Eleonoora."

"A magic spell between our families?"

"Yes."

A voice broke into their conversation. "Liam?" It was Ellie's mother. "Is that you?"

She was headed straight for the nook where he was having dinner with her daughter. Liam faced the open hallway, so Ellie was hidden from view, but in a matter of seconds, Mrs. Thatcher would see them both.

Ellie's eyes widened in alarm. She slid out of her chair and disappeared beneath the long tablecloth.

Liam sought to maintain an impassive face. "Hello, Mrs. Thatcher."

"I'd heard you were back in town. I've been wanting to tell you how sorry I am about your father."

"Thank you."

Her gaze took in the table and the two half-eaten dinners. "I apologize. I didn't mean to interrupt you and your date, but I'm looking for Ellie and Bella. They were having dinner, and my husband's got an upset stomach so we're leaving early. I wanted to see if they need a ride home."

"I'm sure she's around here somewhere," he said. Not exactly a lie.

"I'll keep looking. Will you be at the ball tomorrow? I don't think anyone would be offended if you all skipped it, in deference to your father."

"We're planning to be there. Working on it has helped my mother keep her mind off her grief."

"Understandable. Well, we'll see you then." Then she

added before leaving, her tone a bit conspiratorial, "The feud notwithstanding."

Were the Thatchers tired of the bickering? Had they been nurturing the ill-tempers of two old men as much as his family had? Maybe this feud could finally be put to rest.

Ellie popped her head out and looked up at him. "Is she gone?" she whispered.

"Yes."

"Since when are you friendly with my mother?"

"It's not like our families are strangers. And I'm not going to be rude to her, especially after you told me about her health issues."

She pushed against his leg as she climbed up to her seat. "You need to warn Bella."

When he didn't move fast enough, she nudged him out of his seat.

"All right, all right," he said with a laugh.

He set his napkin on the table and walked quickly to the other nook. Somehow, Mrs. Thatcher had doubled back instead of coming this way since Ryan and Bella looked relaxed as they talked and smiled at one another. That changed the moment Liam appeared.

"Mrs. Thatcher is looking for the girls," he said.

Bella's happy expression immediately shifted to a frown.

"I knew it was a mistake to stay local," Ryan muttered.

"No, it's okay," Bella said, laying a hand on Ryan's arm. "Ellie and I'll just have to go home with them." She stood, grabbing her purse that hung on the corner of the ornate wooden chair.

Liam left them since they probably wanted a minute alone, and his time with Ellie was now down to seconds. But their nook was empty when he returned. He paused, unsure what to do, but then Ellie rushed back in.

"Sorry. I tracked down my mother. I'm afraid I have to go."

"I know. Bella is getting ready too."

"Dinner was delicious. You should box it all up and take it home."

"I'd rather eat it with you."

Without warning, she kissed him, bold and hungry. Wrapping his arms around her, he shifted her out of sight. There was nothing soft and chaste about them finally coming together, the contact escalating quickly to a heat level Liam was unprepared for.

He'd anticipated this going differently—slower and more private—but nothing with Ellie ever seemed to go to plan.

Ellie broke contact first, her breath fast and hot against his lips. A lingering taste of marinara sauce and sexy Ellie remained.

He didn't know what to say.

"There was mistletoe," she whispered, looking as stunned as he felt.

Her eyes flicked upward. A green sprig hung from a hook above their table.

"I'll see you tomorrow," she said, then left him standing alone in the nook, too shocked to speak, a cold wave engulfing him after the loss of her heat.

Bella rushed by a few seconds later, but she didn't look his way.

Liam scrubbed a hand down his face, waiting for his heartbeat to slow to a reasonable rate.

When Ryan joined him, his brother frowned. "What's wrong?"

"I think I've underestimated Ellie Thatcher."

Ryan snapped his fingers in front of Liam's out-of-focus gaze. "Hey, come back to Earth, Liam."

The spell was finally broken, leaving Liam irritated. The vacuum that Ellie's departure had left behind felt like Christmas had been stolen right out from under him.

He wanted it back. He wanted *her* back.

"I can't believe it's taken you so long to realize that you're in love with Ellie."

Love?

But Ryan was right.

Tucking away his disappointment in losing the brightest spot in his day, Liam looked at his brother. "Wanna join me for dinner?"

Ryan grinned. "I thought you'd never ask."

Fifteen

Late Saturday afternoon Ellie arrived at the Barstow Resort, lugging her camera bag on one shoulder while trying to walk like a normal person in the hunter green heels she'd picked especially with Liam in mind. All night her dreams had been filled with him—his smile, his blue eyes watching her with wanting, the feel of his body pressed against hers—and all day she'd been distracted by daydreams of what it would be like if they were alone, really alone. Her body was still humming with excitement. She was beyond hungry to see him.

A very large, fake reindeer greeted her at the entrance. The likeness was quite good, with antlers covered in glitter, and a coat that was white and fluffy, and Ellie stared at it with growing delight in her heart.

The Vaadin.

With a big dose of mirth, Ellie fished her phone out of her coat pocket and snapped a selfie in front of the creature. Maybe Eustace would accept this as evidence? Not likely, but it made Ellie chuckle anyway.

Liam's mother had called her this morning and asked

if she could arrive early to photograph the room and decorations before the guests started arriving, and Ellie had been glad to get out of her parents' house with something to do other than think anxiously about Liam all day.

Since phone calls were tricky between them—there could be other family members around—she and the hot man in question had been exchanging texts, which is how they'd agreed she would come to the ball on her own. Liam was helping his mother by picking up several silent auction items that had been promised at the last minute.

The texts, initiated by Liam this morning, had been … tentative. After the kiss—that kiss! Holy cow, Ellie was still reeling from it—the two of them had talked around it, a giant elephant in the room, as if they'd ignited a firecracker that was poised to go off at any moment.

It was clear there would be no casual dating between them. Was Liam as freaked out as she was? She was afraid to ask.

"Ellie!" Mary Adler beamed as she rounded a corner. Ellie could only hope that Liam's mother would have the same happy expression on her face when Ellie told her she was dating Liam. Because unless Liam got a raging case of cold feet, they were on a collision course for one another. And if last night had shown her anything, it was the difficulty in keeping their red-hot attraction under wraps, with the problem being Ellie herself.

"Hello, Mrs. Adler. You look beautiful."

Liam's mother wore a red pantsuit and shiny black flats. "Thank you. And so do you. Do you have a date joining you later?"

Ellie froze. *Yes, that would be your eldest son.*

"Mary," a woman called from the other room. "We've got a problem with the flowers on the archway. Can you get one of your boys to help?"

Liam was here? Ellie nervously scanned her surroundings.

"They went home to change." Mrs. Adler turned back to Ellie. "You can stash your things in the room off to the right. And after that, please join us in the main ballroom." She hurried off.

Ellie waited a second for her pounding heart to calm itself, since Liam wasn't here. Yet. She took a deep breath and walked to a room filled with several comfortable chairs and a pitcher of water on the coffee table. She poured herself a glass, downed the entire thing, then unpacked her camera gear and headed to the ballroom.

She spent the next hour taking photos as well as helping with decorations for the check-in and auction tables. And then guests began arriving.

Ellie planted herself near the fake Vaadin and was soon guiding arrivals to stand before it for a photo. She snapped pictures of locals she knew and many she didn't, and then Bella and Mason arrived with their parents, Ellie's Uncle Joe and Aunt Sara.

Ellie whispered to Bella, "They're not here yet."

"It's not like we can hang out with them anyway."

"We could take turns in the coat room."

Bella gasped but the idea made her smile. Then she said, "Have you tried my cookies?"

"No."

"Mrs. Adler asked me to make reindeer-themed ones for tonight. I'll grab you one."

Ellie's parents came all dressed up with Owen and Jamie in tow, both in suits, followed by Grandpa Adam and Grandma Isabelle, as well as Nanna. It was a joy to see them all together, and Ellie had them crowd in front of the Vaadin for a photo. She needed to get Bella's family in there as well, so when Bella returned with the cookie, Ellie told her to grab her parents and Mason.

Then she noticed the confection wrapped in the napkin. It was more like a small cake in the shape of a reindeer, covered in white icing and intricate designs in red.

"Bells, this is beautiful. I've never seen you make these before."

"I wanted to do something different, and maybe impress Mrs. Adler a little. I studied Russian Kozuli, a type of rye cookie, and then made it a bit fancier with a gingerbread slant. I was inspired by you."

"By me?"

"These cookies were considered magical talismans that brought wealth, prosperity, and good fortune to the recipients." Bella grinned. "I know how much you like magical things." She pointed to the design. "I wrote different versions of 'reindeer' in Finnish."

Ellie had Bella hold the cookie cake so she could take several photos before finally taking a bite. The spicy sweet flavors melted in her mouth. "This is delicious. You must've added extra magic." She would need to get to the dessert table and grab a few more before they were gone.

She had one of the wait staff take a photo of the entire Thatcher family, then everyone enjoyed a Rudolph spritzer —made of orange and cranberry juices, ginger ale, and a bit of vodka—when a server came by with a trayful. Ellie grabbed one too, hoping it would soothe her nerves as she continued to keep an eye out for Liam.

Jennifer Dixon sidled up to her. "Are you alone after all?" she asked.

"Oh, hi. About that …." This thing with Liam had been weighing on Ellie's conscience, at least when it came to Jennifer, and the right thing was to say something. But the words jammed in her throat and then Jennifer's folks joined them, along with a man who could only be the brother, sharing the same narrow eyes and long nose as his sister.

"This is my brother, David."

Ellie shook his hand. "Nice to meet you."

"You're prettier than Jen said."

Uh-oh. "Thanks." Ellie forced a smile on her face. "How about a photo?"

She herded the Dixons together and took several pictures, and then Jennifer pulled Ellie aside.

"What do you think of David?"

"I … ah …."

"It's not like you have a real date."

Too late, Ellie's mother was nearby and overheard. "You have a date, Ellie?"

"I … ah …."

"Ellie was going with Liam," Jennifer supplied.

Her mom raised a brow. "Liam Adler?"

Jennifer swung her gaze back to Ellie. "Just as friends, right?"

"I … ah …."

And then he was here, standing at the entranceway, wearing a tux, and looking so good that Ellie's mouth hung open. Her heart pounded so fast that she had to take a few extra breaths just to make sure there was enough oxygen in her lungs.

Liam locked eyes with her, and the heat in his eyes was unmistakable.

Several thoughts collided in Ellie's head all at once. Did he like the dress she'd worn? It matched her shoes—green with flowery accents and sparkles and fitted enough to show off her figure. She hadn't wanted Liam to remember the girl she'd been but rather the woman she now was. And then, of course, she needed to explain everything to her mother. And to Jennifer. That she and Liam were supposed to be enemies but instead they were friends.

More than friends.

He walked toward her, and her mind blanked.

"Mrs. Thatcher, you look beautiful," he said.

Ellie's mother smiled but her eyes narrowed with suspicion, and Ellie knew she wasn't buying it, the evidence all but clicking into place inside her mother's head.

"Jennifer, it's good to see you," he said, his tone polite, mollifying. Almost apologetic.

Then he shifted his gaze to Ellie. "Ellie." He didn't say more, but he lingered a smidge too long on her.

She didn't have to look at her mother or Jennifer to know that they knew.

"Liam," Ellie managed to say past the parchment paper her mouth had become. She grabbed her spritzer from a nearby table and took a big gulp.

Thankfully, an influx of arrivals gave Ellie an excuse to avoid any pertinent questions, along with Liam's smoldering glare that was hugely distracting, making her dress feel two sizes too small. His attention was diverted when his grandparents entered with Ryan and Liam's other brother, Flynn. None of them stopped for a photo, saving Ellie the discomfort of small talk.

She pushed through the crowd when she caught sight of Eustace, tugging at the collar of his tuxedo shirt. He'd come with Mark, who had a date Ellie didn't recognize, and Mr. and Mrs. Osborn. Apparently, Jennifer had abandoned her plan to bring him.

Ellie beamed. "I'm so happy to see you, Eustace."

"I was wrangled into coming," he grumbled.

"You look very handsome."

"You deserve to get out of the house once in a while,

Eustace," Mrs. Osborn said. "It's nice to see you again, Ellie."

"Welcome to the ball. May I take your photo?"

Eustace was a bit grumpy, but Ellie soon had the task completed, and then Mark pulled her aside.

"I need to speak with you." He took her arm and led her away before she could protest. More guests were arriving, and he had to push her through the crowd to get to a quiet spot in an adjacent hallway.

"Mark, I have to take photos."

"Why are you trying to undermine the Christmas Village?"

"I'm not. What are you talking about?"

"Some magazine contacted me and said you were working for them. They wanted access to the Village and some background info, except that apparently a company in Finland found out and now they're sending me cease and desist letters about using the Vaadin on promotional items."

Ellie frowned. "Didn't you check all that out before plastering it all over souvenirs?"

"That's beside the point. You and your stupid article about the reindeer around here has caused me a lot of problems."

Liam materialized like a man emerging from a snowstorm. With a hand at Ellie's back, he said, "Is there a problem?"

Mark glared at Liam, then focused on Ellie again. "I think the solution is obvious."

Ellie tried to ignore the heat spreading from Liam's hand. "I'm not following," she said.

"I get Eustace's land."

"Should I be worried about the three of you huddled over here?" Jennifer asked, her face bright with forced joy.

"This isn't up to us," Ellie said to Mark. "It's Eustace's decision."

"I'm filing for a trademark on the Vaadin, and you're going to pay for it." Mark pointed his finger at her.

"No, I'm not," she said.

"C'mon, Mark," Liam said. "I'll buy you a drink, and we can talk about this."

Ellie didn't look at Liam as he guided the other man away, afraid that every emotion she had for him would be written all over her face.

Jennifer surprised her when she said, "Ellie, I had no idea about you and Liam."

"I'm so sorry. I should've told you, but it's very new, and it caught us both by surprise, and …."

Jennifer held up a hand. "It's okay. I'm not mad. Well, maybe a little." But her voice was more teasing than hurt. "He has no interest in me. He's made that abundantly clear." Then she shrugged. "There's still Flynn and Ryan."

Ellie hesitated before saying, "Maybe not Ryan."

Sixteen

Liam made the rounds, visiting with friends of his father as well as acquaintances, making small talk as well as chatting up business. He made sure his mother had a plate of food and a chance to get off her feet, and he danced with his grandmother.

But Ellie was on his mind the entire time. Avoiding her was hell. Watching her from afar in a dress that was sheer distraction was also hell.

He waited all evening for a chance to get her alone. Finally, it arrived during the announcement of the silent auction winners when she slipped out of the ballroom. He stood and followed, catching sight of her just as she entered a room off the outer hallway.

He paused at the closed door. Should he walk in? Should he knock? She might not be alone. What would be his reason for being here? Before he could decide on a course of action, the door swung open, Ellie on the other side.

She startled, then she leaned past him into the hallway, checking for anyone else. Satisfied, she grabbed his arm and pulled him into the room and shut the door. He didn't waste any time and kissed her. She met him with equal fervor, her arms locked around his neck, and her mouth slanted against his.

He'd been thinking about her all day, about what it would be like to have her close. The reality was better.

The kisses became hungrier, his hands moving of their own accord. With great reluctance, he pulled back and she groaned in protest.

"You're supposed to be my date," she whispered.

"I don't think I can keep the way I feel about you a secret if I'm near you. Everyone will know."

"My mom suspects. Jennifer knows."

"She does?"

"Sorry about that."

"No, it's okay. But she probably won't keep it to herself."

Ellie kissed him, then said, "Probably not. But you should warn Flynn. I don't want to hurt your pride, but she's on the prowl for an Adler, and it seems any Adler will do."

"She wants Flynn?" He laughed. "He's married."

"Since when?"

"Last summer. He and his wife eloped."

"I had no idea. Is she here?"

"No," he said. "She's coming on Christmas Eve."

A knock on the door made them both jump apart. Someone from the wait staff came in. "I didn't mean to interrupt," she said. "I just need to switch the water pitchers."

Liam nodded while Ellie was patting her hair that had become loose from her bun during their hot and heavy encounter.

When they were alone again, Ellie took a deep breath. "We should probably get back out there."

"Can I see you later?"

"How?"

"We'll figure something out."

Ellie left the sitting room about five minutes after Liam, giving her time to compose herself. If they hadn't been interrupted, she and Liam might have kept going and ....

Avoiding her family's table, she went to the buffet and filled a plate with ham, sweet potatoes, honey-glazed carrots, cornbread stuffing, and cranberry sauce. She had continued to photograph attendees and had missed the chance to eat earlier. Her stomach had been in knots anyway, but the steamy encounter with Liam had released that tension, so her hunger had sprung to life.

She headed for Eustace sitting at a table by himself, a plate of roast beef and mashed potatoes before him.

"Can I join you?" she asked.

He waved her to the seat beside him. "Please do."

Once settled, she asked, "No gravy?"

"Never been a fan." He took a drink of something creamy that looked like eggnog.

"I wanted to ask you something." She placed a cloth napkin on her lap. "Do you think it's possible that my great-great grandmother had a special connection to her reindeer? Like some sort of reindeer whisperer?"

"My pappy said she was known to have a way with the animals."

"Could she have placed some sort of blessing over the herd that she and her father brought here? That there was a sacred pact between the reindeer, Charlie Thatcher, and

Henry Adler? If I'm translating her journal correctly, the pact should never be broken."

Eustace cut the roast beef with his knife and fork. "What are you getting at?"

"When my grandfather and Liam's fought over Grandma Isabelle, and my grandpa gave all the deer to Theo Adler, then maybe the pact was broken."

"Does she mention the Vaadin?"

She nodded. "She said what you'd said, that if a couple witnesses the Vaadin then it's true love. When you and your wife saw it, was it before or after my grandfather gave the herd to Theo?"

"It was before."

"What about my grandparents?"

"Also before, I believe." Eustace became contemplative. "So, the pact was broken and the Vaadin was never seen again. You make a good detective, Ellie."

"Or maybe I have a good imagination." She smashed one of the sweet potatoes onto a piece of ham and ate them together.

Eustace chewed a bite of his food, then said, "It might help if Theo and Adam could bury their animosity and share the herd once again."

"Restore balance to the universe?" she teased. "I think you're asking too much."

With the silent auction ended, the guests had started mingling at the dessert table and filling the dance floor. Ellie found the men in question on opposite sides of the room, each beside his wife.

Liam's voice sounded behind her. "Good evening, Eustace." Then he caught her gaze. "I was hoping for a dance, but we've got a problem. Mick just called. Lumi escaped her stall and has run off."

"Oh no."

"Is that the one you tried to pass off as the Vaadin?" Eustace asked.

Ellie nodded. "Something must've spooked her."

"Or called her," Eustace said. "Today is the Winter Solstice, the longest night of the year. Did you know that in ancient folklore this night was called Mother Night? The origins of Santa Claus are rooted in a very female story, that of the Deer Mother who flew across the skies, drawn by her most faithful female reindeer, and carrying the light of the sun in her horns to illuminate the darkness. In fact, in some tales, she threw pebbles of amber into chimneys, symbolizing the sun."

"Are you saying that Lumi has gone into the mountains to look for her herd?" Liam asked.

"Maybe they know she's here and have been calling her."

"Mick is worried she's too domesticated and won't survive in the wild," Liam said. "I'm not sure if he'll buy your magical tale."

"It's not for anyone to buy. But I would like to go home."

"You think she'll go that high?" Ellie asked.

"It might help to leave an offering."

"Such as?" Liam asked.

"Lichen. Mushrooms. I have some on hand. But there are pathways in those mountains, used by the wild reindeer, and even your Adler herds. Your Lumi will know them."

"How?" Ellie asked.

"Reindeer see much that we can't."

"I'm going to head up there and help Mick and his team search," Liam said.

Ellie stood. "I'll come too."

Eustace looked at each of them. “Can you give me a ride?”

Seventeen

Liam dropped Ellie off at her parents' house so she could change clothes while he went home to do the same. Eustace stayed in the front seat of the SUV, listening to Christmas music on the radio and munching on a candy cane.

Once Ellie was tucked back into the car, Liam drove to Eustace's cabin. The sky was dark and clear, revealing a vast display of twinkling stars. Ellie had her best winter gear and a backpack with supplies. Liam had the same. He'd been on the phone with Mick, telling the farm manager they were headed high while Mick and the others searched from the bottom of the valley and up. If they were lucky, they'd find Lumi somewhere in the middle. Mick thought she'd escaped several hours ago, so she could've covered a lot of distance since then. It was entirely possible she was near Eustace's property, following ancient pathways if the old man was to be believed.

They stopped at Eustace's cabin and went inside, greeted by Lilja.

"Take her with you," Eustace said. "She's got a good nose for reindeer."

"But it's too cold," Ellie said, on her knees and enjoying an onslaught of face-licks and happy bounces from the dog.

"She's got booties and her fleece jacket." He retrieved them from a basket near the front door.

Liam helped Ellie get everything on the dog, who wagged her tail the entire time, oblivious to the ministrations.

"Any advice on where to go?" Liam asked as he shouldered his pack.

"Just past the ridgeline there's a sheltered meadow. I'm an old man and haven't been back there in years, but the local reindeer could be found there back in my younger days."

"The Arctic herd?" Ellie asked.

Eustace shrugged.

Ellie gasped. "Eustace, have they been out here the entire time? Have you always known?"

"They'll be seen if they want to be seen."

"We were in that meadow last week," Liam said. "There was no sign of any herds."

Eustace waved at them to follow him to his shed where he retrieved a canvas bag. "Take this. It might attract them."

It was the lichen and mushrooms he'd mentioned earlier. Liam put the pouch in his backpack.

"Stay safe," Eustace added. "I'll put out more food in case they come by here."

Ellie produced a flashlight from her pack and they headed out, Lilja bounding beside them.

❄

After four hours of searching, Ellie was exhausted. And cold. Which meant Lilja had to be ready for a break as well.

They'd found nothing and it was disheartening, although being alone with Liam was an unexpected treat.

"We need a break," she said.

"You're right."

"We're not far from Eleonoora's cabin."

"Lead the way."

Her watch said three a.m. when they finally spotted it through the trees. As they approached, Liam dropped a pile of lichen and mushrooms.

Once inside, Ellie lit a lamp with matches, the action familiar. As Liam took in all the changes, his face registered shock.

"You did all this?" he asked.

She grinned with pride. Aside from the deep clean, she'd added a full-size air mattress, pillows and two sleeping bags rated at minus ten degrees Fahrenheit zipped together. She'd crashed on the bed a few times when she'd been here late. She'd brought a comfy dog bed for Lilja, as well as wood for the stove, which was now in working order. There was food—nothing fancy, just some nuts, granola bars, and beef jerky, and a case of water that had been a bear to lug. Unfortunately, it kept freezing when she wasn't here. She'd left a good pair of binoculars sitting on a table near the front window as well as a sturdy tripod for her camera.

Liam met her gaze. "Have you been living here?"

"Just camping out when I was trying to get photos. The regular reindeer have come by several times. Maybe their scent will attract Lumi."

Liam went to work making a fire while Ellie gave Lilja water from the bottle she'd brought with her. She also poured a cup of kibble into a bowl, having stocked both when it became clear that anytime Ellie was here, Lilja somehow knew and made the trek from Eustace's to join her.

As the heat from the burning wood began chasing away the chill, Lilja investigated the smells of the room, then collapsed onto her bed and promptly went to sleep.

"She's beat," Ellie said, joining Liam by the stove.

"Lilja's not the only one. Why don't you try to get some rest."

"Any word from Mick?" Worry gnawed at her over Lumi's disappearance, but the girl was big and strong. A Colorado winter night would be nothing compared to Lapland. She should be fine.

"Not since the last call, when they lost that promising trail south of the farm."

Ellie glanced at Liam's profile in the soft orange light from the stove. "It's been quite a day."

"A long one." He gave her a small smile, but he hadn't made a move to kiss her.

She resisted the urge to reach out to him. "Liam, do you think we're a good idea?"

His eyes narrowed, showing more amusement than worry. "Having doubts, Thatcher?"

"We won't be able to date like normal people. At least, not in Reindeer Pass."

"You're far from normal, Ellie."

"Thanks. I think."

"Maybe we're fate."

She let out a mock gasp. "Liam Adler, are you starting to believe in magic?"

"I do when I look at you."

He reached up to push a strand of hair from her face,

the gesture gentle and filled with possibility, the brush of his hand igniting a fire in her abdomen.

There had been other boyfriends, she was even still friends with a few, but everything about Liam—while familiar in so many ways—was different. Even the air between them was heavy with what she could only call inevitability. As if she had always been meant for Liam, and he for her.

"You're beautiful, Ellie."

"There won't be any going back after this," she whispered. "If this doesn't work, one of us will have to leave the state."

He ran his thumb along her lower lip, and she shivered.

"I really don't think that's going to be a problem," he said.

The kiss was soft and tender, an exploration of one another they'd missed out on in the first two encounters. With their winter gear impeding more body contact, their lips were the only connection, and Ellie savored it.

She held onto his wrists as his hands cupped the sides of her face, the kiss deepening, unleashing the longing she'd done her best to keep contained the past few days. Matching his hunger, she was soon overheated. And not just from the fire.

She unzipped her coat and shed it.

He did the same, saying against her lips as she reached for him again, "Ellie, we don't have to rush this."

"I know. But how often will we find ourselves alone?"

He held her still. "Are you sure?"

"Are you?"

"If we move forward, we'll have to tell the family."

She groaned and gave him a playful shove. "Are you *trying* to kill my desire?"

He tugged her close. "Of course not."

She wrapped her arms around his neck and smiled as she proceeded to kiss him senseless. Then she started tugging at his clothing.

He caught her hands in his. "Wait. Protection. I don't have any."

She pushed his Henley up. "Don't worry. I'm covered."

He pulled the shirt over his head. His t-shirt came next. Ellie enjoyed the view of his bare torso, lean and muscular, giving a heady dose of reality to everything she had imagined, and she ran her hands over him. Her layers of clothing came next.

Her spontaneity surprised her, but her need to get closer to Liam consumed her. She had never been so impulsive with a guy, so ravenous, as if he were the oxygen she needed to live. He laid claim to her with the same greediness, stringing her so tight that when she came, she nearly cried.

He held her fiercely, his possession absolute, whispering her name as she arched against him. She clung to him, loving the weight of him on her, the strength of his body, the warmth of his breath, and the focus with which he made love. The crest of pleasure lingered, and she sighed.

"You've been hiding your magical powers, Liam."

He brought his mouth to hers, laughing softly. "No regrets?"

"Only that we waited so long to do this."

"I want more than a fling with you, Ellie."

"You're funny," she joked. "That you ever thought this would be a fling."

Eighteen

Lilja's barking awoke Liam with a start, and Ellie stirred in his arms. They were tucked into the sleeping bag, and he'd slept deeply with Ellie's naked body pressed against his.

It was still dark, and a faint amber glow emanated from the stove, so he hadn't slept more than an hour at most. Men's voices outside jolted him more fully awake.

"Ellie," he whispered. "Someone's here." She mumbled in protest. With regret he left her warmth and began searching for clothing on the floor. Ellie left the sleeping bag slowly and stood, her bare silhouette in the muted light stirring him back to life. He forced himself to look away.

Liam jammed his legs into his jeans and barely had his t-shirt on when bootsteps sounded on the porch. Ellie squealed as she quickly covered herself with the bare minimum—long-sleeved shirt and long john bottoms.

Liam ran a hand through his hair as the door swung open, a flashlight blinding him. He shielded his eyes as Lilja's loud and incessant barking filled the air.

"Liam!"

"Gramps?" The cold blast of air chilled Liam's bare feet.

"Ellie?" It was Adam Thatcher.

Liam inwardly groaned. Both he and Ellie were both about to catch hell.

"What in God's name is going on?" Mr. Thatcher demanded.

"Is this some sort of love nest?" Gramps' voice was filled with accusation.

Liam almost laughed at the odds of these two men joining together to come here, which by all accounts should've been zero. Then he caught sight of Ellie's lacy bra lying near the rumpled sleeping bag.

"Could you both lower your flashlights?" Ellie said. "And please close the door. You're letting in all the cold air."

They did as she said as she shushed Lilja, and Liam took the opportunity to push the bra out of sight with his toe.

"Look," Liam said. "I say this with the utmost respect. Ellie and I are adults. We can do what we want."

Mr. Thatcher frowned. "Then why are you hiding out here in this broken-down shack?"

"Because they've gone explicitly behind our backs," Gramps said, shaking his head. "Liam, really? A Thatcher?"

Mr. Thatcher turned to the man beside him. "What the hell are you saying, Theo? We don't have the plague. I'm the one who should be affronted. Liam seduced her."

"That's enough," Ellie interjected. "If anything, *I* seduced Liam."

Liam couldn't stop the smile tugging at the corners of his mouth, so he looked down to hide it.

Her statement had left the grandfathers speechless, so

she continued. "You two really need to get over yourselves because Liam and I are planning to …." She looked at Liam with a question in her eyes, then she shrugged. "Date?"

Liam smiled. "Absolutely."

Mr. Thatcher sighed, then said, "Are you happy, Ellie?"

She grinned, her eyes locked on Liam. "Yes. Very."

It felt like Christmas morning to Liam, leaving him dazed and excited about what was to come.

Ellie crossed her arms. "What are you both doing here in the middle of the night?"

"Looking for you," Gramps replied. "We heard about that damned reindeer escaping, and you kids running off after her. It's dangerous in these mountains, especially at night."

"You both came together?" Liam asked.

The men exchanged a glance. "We were worried," Mr. Thatcher said. "It seemed prudent to stick together. We stopped at Eustace's, and he told us about the cabin."

"Haven't you ever been here?" Ellie asked.

Mr. Thatcher glanced around. "We have. It was a long time ago, wasn't it, Theo?"

Gramps let out a huff then waved a hand between Liam and Ellie. "What is this? Is there a wedding happening soon?"

"Give us a chance to get to know one another," Liam answered.

"It looks like you two *have* gotten to know each other," Gramps said. "Too well." He sighed and turned to Mr. Thatcher. "We'll split the wedding cost."

Ellie's grandfather nodded. "I'll agree to that."

"Hold on," Ellie said. "You both are moving a little fast. And besides, there'll be no wedding with you two feuding."

"So now you expect us to bury the hatchet?" Gramps demanded.

Ellie put her hands on her hips. "Yes. I understand how hard it must've been when my grandmother chose Grandpa over you, but don't you think you can forgive him after all this time?"

"Is that why you think I'm mad?"

The three of them stared at Theo Adler in silence, including Lilja, who had given up her sniffing of the strangers and had returned to her bed by the fire.

"Well, of course I was mad about that at the time," Gramps continued, dismissing it with a wave, then glanced at Mr. Thatcher. "But then you gave me your half of the reindeer and … that told me enough." He looked away. "You thought our friendship was over."

Mr. Thatcher's face registered shock. "But it was."

Gramps simply nodded, swallowing thickly.

"What are you saying, Gramps?" Liam said, surprised to see such vulnerability in his grandfather. He generally worked hard to keep people away. "Do you want to be friends with Adam?"

Gramps cleared his throat. "Of course I do. It was clear to me not long after Izzy chose you that you two were better suited, that she was happier. I made peace with that. And then I met Charlotte, and I was blessed. She's put up with me all these years, but I'm the lucky one. I'm positive that Izzy and I could've never been that for each other." He took a breath, clearly uncomfortable. "What hurt more was that I lost our friendship." He glanced at Adam Thatcher. "You abandoned the deer to me."

"I wanted to make amends. You loved the reindeer, and everything that had been built by our ancestors. I felt great pain when I fell in love with Izzy, because I never wanted to hurt you. I tried to fight it, but it was bigger than the both of us. I wanted to give you something of equal value, although of course it wasn't, but it was all I could offer at the time. But God knows I've missed you, and the reindeer." He paused, then said, his voice thick with emotion, "I've missed my friend all these years."

Gramps went silent, and Liam thought his tough, feisty grandfather might cry.

"Well, then." Gramps cleared his throat with a laugh. "We've made a muck of things, haven't we, Adam?"

"I suppose we have. I'm sorry about Izzy. You must know that."

"I know," Theo replied. "And I'm sorry I've hogged the reindeer all these years. But that hasn't kept your granddaughter from loitering on my properties."

Ellie smiled.

Gramps shifted his attention to Liam. "Do you love her?"

Yes. But he didn't want to scare Ellie with an admission too soon.

"Mr. Adler," Ellie said. "You shouldn't put Liam on the spot like that. I don't need things to move quickly."

"Fine." He turned back to Ellie's grandfather. "We'll also split the cash bar at the reception."

"Agreed," Adam said.

Ellie cast an exasperated look at Liam, but then she laughed, and he relaxed. She wasn't scared off. And maybe, just maybe, their grandfathers would be able to get along going forward.

Thinking it was probably best to get it all out in the open, Liam said, "You should also know that Ryan and Bella Thatcher …."

Gramps and Mr. Thatcher stared at him with a stunned, confused silence, like he'd just told them they were both broke. Their glares were even more menacing since their faces were in partial shadow from the glow of the flashlights.

"Ah, hell," Gramps said. "We're gonna be related one way or another, Adam."

"Looks that way. It's not such a bad thing, is it Theo?"

Gramps' face softened. "Nah, I suppose not. It'll be nice to have some great-grandkids."

Liam wanted to correct them, to say that he and Ellie were nowhere close to a discussion of marriage, but then Ellie shushed them all. A bright glow was spilling through the window.

"What the …." Gramps opened the door as Ellie jammed her boots onto her feet and grabbed her coat.

Liam didn't have time to stop her before she bolted for the doorway.

But she forgot to duck.

Nineteen

Ellie opened her eyes, night sky above her and dense pine trees crowding close. How did she get here?

She pushed upright, sitting atop a bed of pine needles that insulated her from the snowy ground. Familiarity tugged at Ellie. Eleonoora had described this place in her journal, where she'd often gone to speak to the reindeer. Ellie hadn't believed it was real and had wondered if she was mistranslating, or if maybe Eleonoora was speaking more from imagination. Or dreams perhaps. The phrase *where myth meets magic* had played in Ellie's mind as she'd read these parts of the journal.

She stood and dusted twigs and snow from her coat and hair, a tingle down her spine making her aware she was being watched.

As if conjured from Ellie's own mind, the Arctic herd became visible in the trees one by one. Holding her breath, Ellie spun in a slow circle, a glow from each animal's eyes pinpointing their location. They surrounded her, magnificent and calm.

The largest one came forward, antlers reaching to the sky and hooves the size of small tires. Was it Lumi? But this reindeer was much grander. She could only be the Vaadin, the Reindeer Goddess.

Knowing filled Ellie's mind—of all that had come before, of Eleonoora's deep and abiding love not only to the reindeer but to her husband, Charlie Thatcher, and to their children, Ellie's ancestors. True love came in all facets, not just romantic.

Beside the Vaadin was an old canvas bag, and Ellie knew it had been Eleonoora's. Ellie knelt and opened it. Inside was an old cloth with the likeness of a reindeer with massive antlers that held the sun, a silver chain with a reindeer medallion, and a small drum made of deer hide.

Ellie began to beat the drum tentatively, and then her confidence grew. One after another, the reindeer, their hides glowing white from the illumination from the Vaadin, took flight. The tales of Santa's reindeer had been based on fact after all.

Finally, it was only Ellie and the Vaadin in the small clearing, and Ellie stopped drumming. The magical reindeer came to her and kneeled, the offering clear. Filled with nervous excitement, Ellie set the drum and canvas bag aside. She climbed onto the animal's back and grabbed the antlers for stability. The Vaadin rose to her full height, then trotted forward and leapt into the air, taking to the sky, rising higher and higher. Ellie laughed, filled with awe. And love.

Eustace had been right. Before there had been Santa Claus, there had been the ancient Deer Mother, the first to fly across the winter skies, bringing light to the land that had been cast into darkness. The rising sun flashed on the horizon, bathing the land in an amber glow.

Eleonoora had known this. Now Ellie did too.

❄

"Ellie. Ellie!"

She opened her eyes. Liam's worried face came into view. She was on the air mattress surrounded by Liam, the grandfathers, and Lilja.

"You hit your head," Liam said.

"Knocked you clean out," Mr. Adler said. "Never saw anything like it."

Ellie touched her forehead, wincing. "She was here."

"Who?" her grandfather asked.

"The Vaadin. Did you see her?"

"There was a strange glow outside," Liam said. "But then you went down, and we were worried you were hurt."

She tried to rise but flinched at the pain in her head. Outside the window was darkness. Had she imagined it all?

"We're taking you to the hospital right now," Grandpa said.

"No arguing, girl," Mr. Adler insisted.

"But Lumi …." Ellie said. "We still don't know where she is."

Liam gently smoothed back her hair. "We'll keep looking. Please let us take you to the hospital first."

She wanted to share what she'd experienced, but the words hovered just beyond reach. Had it all been a dream?

She gripped Liam's arm, pulling him to her, and he gently kissed her.

He wasn't a dream. Thank goodness.

He was here, and they were together.

And she loved him. She'd always loved him.

She nodded. "Okay."

❄

Ellie sat at Eustace's kitchen table, Liam with her as they sipped tea and ate gingerbread cookies that Bella had made. She was sporting a big bruise on her forehead from where she'd collided with the doorframe three nights ago, but otherwise the doctors had said she was fine. She wore her old red knit hat with Rudolph and *OH DEER!* on it to hide the injury. No reason to worry the old man.

"Still no sign of Lumi?" she asked.

"No," Eustace replied, but his focus was directed at Liam. "She'll be all right. These mountains have places where the reindeer can thrive. Places away from humans."

Ellie's heart sank. "She's not coming back, is she?"

Eustace gave a slight shrug and munched on his cookie.

She'd told Liam everything that had happened after hitting her head, and he'd believed her, and then he'd surprised her when he urged her to share it with Eustace.

Where to start? Best to just jump in.

"There was a glowing light …."

Eustace waited.

"Was it …?"

He nodded. "The Vaadin."

"But we didn't really see anything," she said. Liam and the grandfathers had been solely focused on her, their backs turned from the doorway and whatever had illuminated the meadow in front of the cabin.

"Who saw the glow?" Eustace asked.

"Liam, me, and our grandfathers."

"Hmm. Are they still feuding?"

"No," she said. "In fact, right before that they'd made up."

Eustace's eyebrows shot up in surprise. "Really? What prompted that?"

Liam smiled and moved his arm to rest on the back of

Ellie's chair. "They were planning my and Ellie's wedding."

Delight filled Eustace's gaze as Lilja's tail rapped against the floor beside them. Then he said, "A common goal broke through the animosity. Sounds like true love all around."

It was true. Ellie could feel it in her heart, but she didn't want to jinx what she and Liam had by assuming too much too soon. Or that maybe Theo and Adam wouldn't start arguing again. Time would tell for both.

She proceeded to describe her encounter with the magical reindeer to Eustace. Had it been somewhere in the woods nearby? Or had it been in a place removed, an enchanted *somewhen?*

"What do you think?" she asked quietly when she had finished.

"I'm not sure, but what I do know is that it's you. You're the one."

"The one for what?"

"I knew the land was somewhat broken, I just wasn't sure the cause or the solution. But it's you, and your connection to Eleonoora, and the bond you both have with the reindeer that will heal it. You've already begun by uniting the Adlers and the Thatchers, not just with your grandfathers, but with you two." His gaze included Liam. "I believe the Vaadin will come to you again, in much more glory. Be patient. In the meantime, my property is yours."

Joy filled her heart. "I would be honored, Eustace, but I'm not sure how I'll pay for it."

"We'll work something out," he said, a twinkle in his eye.

Liam's hand moved to her shoulder with a light squeeze, quietly lending his support.

Eustace dusted crumbs from his hands and stood. “It’s Christmas Eve, and I’ve got work to do at the Christmas Village. It’s still Santa Claus the people want to see. But maybe, one day with the Vaadin’s help, we’ll honor the Deer Mother once again. Just as Eleonoora did.”

Ellie jumped to her feet, startling Lilja, and gave Eustace a hug.

“Can we join you?” she asked. “I’ll bring my camera.”

“Make sure you get my good side.”

Twenty

One Year Later

Ellie swayed in Liam's arms enjoying the final dance at their wedding reception at the Barstow Resort. It had been an emotional ceremony followed by a blow-out party—paid for by their grandfathers—but now Ellie was enjoying holding her husband close, without worrying about hiding her love because of a family feud.

"How long before Bella says yes to this?" Liam said, his lips at Ellie's temple.

"I think she wanted to let us go first," she said. "Pave the way."

She met his gaze and he kissed her, long and slow. Surrounded by couples, Ellie didn't feel conspicuous, and she leaned into him.

"I think it's time to go," he murmured.

She smiled. "We have time. Our room is here at the resort."

"Actually no. I cancelled it. We're going to Eleonoora's cabin. I hope you don't mind. Since it's the Winter Solstice, I thought you'd like to be there. Maybe …."

Ellie knew what he was thinking. "Lumi."

The past year had been filled with many highs—she'd purchased Eustace's land with help from her grandfather and had moved into his cabin with Lilja, forgoing the condo that her father had tried to get her into; her photography business was growing; and her relationship with Liam had quickly turned serious. But they'd never found Lumi. For all the time that Ellie spent in the mountains in her new home, she had seen no sign of any Arctic reindeer, although several times she'd come across a trail of unique hoofprints. Per Eustace's instructions, she regularly left out offerings of lichen and mushrooms, but whatever was eating it had eluded detection.

A shadow crossed Liam's face, and Ellie's heart squeezed. Losing Lumi had been like losing his dad again, and while he didn't talk of it much, she knew he felt terrible about never finding her, despite repeated attempts by him and Mick to search for her.

"Let's go to the cabin," she whispered, kissing him again.

An hour later, after many goodbyes and hugs from her parents and Liam's mother, Liam's brothers, her brothers, her aunt and uncle and Bella, her maid of honor, they'd been pulled aside by the grandfathers.

Theo Adler handed her an envelope.

"What's this?" she said.

"An exchange of sorts."

Inside was a document deeding the reindeer farm to Liam and Ellie Adler. While she had relished the fact that as an Adler she would have a link to the farm, she'd never thought she would be an owner.

Emotion clogged her throat. "I don't know what to say." She hugged Theo. "Thank you!"

"You're part of the family now," he said, releasing her. "And I suspect no one loves that farm more than you do." Then he turned to Adam. "Can you top that for a wedding gift?"

Her grandfather laughed. "Theo, I already did. I gave my granddaughter to the Adler family. I'd say my debt for having taken Isabelle from you is repaid."

"I suppose that sounds fair," Theo grumbled.

The two men still argued from time to time, but the decades-long rift in their friendship was slowly healing, and Ellie was glad for it.

"You'd better take care of her," Grandpa Adam said to Liam.

"I will, sir." Liam clasped his hand.

"All right," Theo said. "We need to let these two lovebirds leave. They don't need to spend their wedding night in the company of two old men. Let's have a nightcap, Adam, in honor of this most unusual union."

Ellie hugged them both, and Liam did the same, and then she left with her husband.

When she and Liam arrived at the cabin, he scooped her up from the SUV and carried her through the much-enlarged doorway, which Liam had insisted on during the renovations she'd done. "In case you bolt out the door again," he'd said. They'd also insulated the walls and installed indoor plumbing.

"Lilja!" Ellie exclaimed once they were inside.

The dog was supposed to be staying with Liam's brother Flynn and his wife at a rental in town. She planted a quick kiss on her husband then landed on her feet to embrace the second love of her life.

"Hi, sweetheart," she cooed as Lilja greeted her with happy abandon. "How'd she get here?"

"I had Flynn bring her, and a few other things."

There was champagne on the small kitchen table and a fire glowing in the new pipe stove, along with fresh food and water for the dog.

"This is wonderful," she said. "Thank you."

He opened the bubbly and filled the accompanying flutes, and they clicked the glasses together.

"To Eleanor Thatcher Adler," he said. "You have miraculously brought our two families together."

"You're welcome," she teased. With a grin, she sipped the champagne, then lifted the hem of her wedding gown and scooted onto the kitchen table, her legs dangling. She kicked off her satin white heels.

Liam didn't miss the invitation, taking her flute and setting both off to the side. He pushed her gown up and stepped between her legs, kissing her, hot and hungry, and their impatience had him take her right there while still in their wedding attire.

As they panted to catch their breath, Ellie said, "That was probably the fastest marriage consummation in history."

"It was your fault." He nipped a path along the side of her neck. "You know better than to jump on the table."

"True." They'd had a few steamy rendezvous here already. It was a good thing they'd bought a sturdy set. "Take me to bed, then."

He obeyed, dutifully freeing her from her long-sleeved gown with at least fifty buttons down the backside. Then he made love to her, much slower and more thoroughly, on the new bed that had replaced the air mattress months ago.

Later Ellie awoke, Liam behind her and his arm hooked around her waist. Lilja snored quietly from her dog bed near the stove.

She shifted and Liam murmured, "You're not thinking of getting up, are you, Mrs. Adler?"

Her new married status was going to take some getting used to. Liam's hands began to roam, and since they were both still naked, she was about to succumb to his sleepy, sexy charm when she noticed a glow outside the window.

"Liam!" She pushed at him to get his attention. "Look!"

Before he could respond, she threw back the covers.

"Do I have any clothes?" she asked. Her wedding dress was draped over a chair, but it would be impossible to get back into it quickly.

He pointed to the corner where a duffle bag sat. She found everything she needed and was soon bundled up in jeans and layers of fleece. As she tied her boots, Liam went to the window and let out a low whistle.

"What is it?" she asked, briefly distracted by his bared body, all beauty and muscle, and her happiness burned bright. He was all hers.

As she rushed to the window, Lilja jumped up and started a low, repetitive bark that she reserved for deer and elk. And maybe reindeer?

The meadow in front of the cabin was all aglow, but the source wasn't clear. Ellie grabbed her camera bag and quickly assembled a lens and camera, while Liam threw on clothing.

"Lilja, stay," she said, as she slipped out the door, closing it behind her. She didn't want the dog to scare anything off. With hope it wasn't something else, like a bear.

The eerie illumination reminded her of this same night

a year ago when she'd hit her head and gone flying with the Reindeer Goddess. Liam joined her on the porch, Lilja still adamantly barking from inside.

He put a knit hat on his head, then planted her red Reindeer one on hers. "Shall we check it out?" he asked.

With anticipation, she nodded and snapped a few photos before they crept down the steps and around the side of the house where she normally left the lichen.

They both skidded to a stop. Shimmering before them was a large, ethereal white reindeer.

"Is it a ghost?" Liam said, his voice low.

"No. It's the Vaadin."

It all made sense now, how the Vaadin continued to appear to couples more than a hundred years later.

"A Christmas spirit?" he asked.

"I think she's more than that. She's the spirit of all reindeer. The Reindeer Mother."

Then the apparition dissolved before them, and Ellie gasped. Before them was a herd of reindeer, their fur as white as snow. There were at least twenty animals, several with large antlers.

"The Arctic herd," Ellie said filled with awe. Then she remembered her camera and started snapping photos, kicking herself for not getting proof of the Vaadin to show Eustace.

The herd stepped aside and from the fog of the forest came another reindeer, this one tall and majestic. A queen among them, completely undeterred by Lilja's muted barking from inside the cabin.

Reverence filled Ellie's voice. "It's Lumi."

"She's alive."

Ellie took his hand and squeezed it. He'd been more heartbroken than he'd ever admitted over losing the gift from his father.

"She looks amazing," Ellie said. "She's obviously managed to thrive." Tears streamed down her face. "She's found her place."

"I think you're right."

Lumi assumed a regal position of authority, then she pawed at the ground revealing a canvas bag near her hooves.

"Did she bring something?" Liam asked.

Ellie started to move forward, but Liam grabbed her arm. "We don't know how she'll react," he said. "You could get hurt."

But Ellie knew that Lumi wouldn't harm her. She could almost hear the creature's thoughts. Is this how it had been for Eleonoora?

Ellie looked at Liam. "I think she has something for me. It'll be okay."

Liam hesitated, then agreed with a reluctant nod.

Ellie approached Lumi. The rest of the herd backed away, but Lumi calmly held her ground.

"Hi, girl." When Ellie was near, Lumi took a step back, allowing Ellie to retrieve the bag. It was the same one that had been in her vision a year ago, the one that had belonged to Eleonoora.

Lumi turned and walked into the woods. Holding the bag, Ellie followed, the crunch of Liam's boots signaling his presence behind her.

A full moon lit the way, and Ellie managed to snap more photos as she walked, landing on a path that she hadn't seen before. A rocky escarpment blocked the way, but Lumi knew a way around it.

As they entered a protected area surrounded by a tight cluster of trees, Ellie felt a chill of recognition. This place had been in her vision after she'd hit her head. She'd met the Vaadin here and had flown the skies with her.

Lumi stopped and bobbed her head, then made eye contact with Ellie. Following the direction the reindeer faced, Ellie could see bones lying beneath a pine tree.

"She brought you here," Liam said. "Why would she do that?"

"For this." Ellie pointed at the remains, then knelt to inspect them. "These are the bones of the original female reindeer that Eleonoora brought. The first Arctic girl. When she passed, she became spirit, and now she's part of the Vaadin, appearing to those who have a true connection. A soul bond."

"Like the grandfathers?"

"And us."

"You always believed, Ellie. I think that's what I love about you the most."

She stood and moved into his arms, burying her face against his neck. "You believed, too. You just didn't know it. I love you, Liam."

"I love you too, Ellie."

Under the watchful eye of Lumi, they began their life together.

Don't miss "The Reindeer That Got Away," a digital prequel short story about Liam and Ellie. Find more info at kmccaffrey.com/the-reindeer-that-got-away/

A Cowboy Christmas Novella

A second-chance romance ...

In high school, she had been quiet and wickedly smart, both a determined tomboy and a girly-girl, a combination that was uniquely Skye. She had always caught his eye but for his own self-preservation, he'd stayed away from her, even when she'd made a play for him.

Skye Mallory has always aspired to leave her family's ranch, and she takes pride in having achieved her dream of becoming a lawyer. But when an unexpected inheritance draws her home for the Christmas holidays, she's surprised by a longing to set down roots in the wide-open meadows and woodlands of southwestern Colorado.

Only one thing stands in her way—a cowboy who broke her heart nine years ago.

In high school, Joe Carrigan admired Skye for her spirit and intellect, but he knew she was destined for a life beyond ranching. Turning down her romantic overture was the best course of action for them both. But now, he's returned to their hometown, and it's inevitable he'll come face-to-face with his one regret in life—Skye Mallory. This time, however, he won't be so chivalrous.

Learn more at
kmccaffrey.com/the-peppermint-tree/

About the Author

Kristy McCaffrey has been writing since she was very young, but it wasn't until she was a stay-at-home mom that she considered becoming published. A fascination with science led her to earn two mechanical engineering degrees—she did her undergraduate work at Arizona State University and her graduate studies at the University of Pittsburgh—but storytelling has always been her passion. She writes both contemporary adventures and award-winning historical western romances.

An Arizona native, Kristy and her husband reside in the desert where they frequently remove (rescue) rattlesnakes from their property, go for runs among the cactus, and plan trips to far-off places like the Orkney Islands or Machu Picchu. But mostly, she works 12-hour days and enjoys at-home date nights with her sweetheart, which usually include Will Ferrell movies and sci-fi flicks. Her four children have all flown the nest, so she lavishes her maternal instincts on Jeb, an American Bulldog her family rescued in 2021. He has his own Instagram account at @jeb_therescue.

Connect with Kristy

Website: kmccaffrey.com
Newsletter: kmccaffrey.com/subscribe
Facebook: facebook.com/AuthorKristyMcCaffrey
Instagram: instagram.com/kristymccaffreybooks
BookBub: bookbub.com/authors/kristy-mccaffrey
TikTok: tiktok.com/@kristymccaffrey

www.ingramcontent.com/pod-product-compliance
Lightning Source LLC
Chambersburg PA
CBHW072227190626
46809CB00017B/1363

* 9 7 8 1 9 5 2 8 0 1 3 4 1 *